G.

Books in
The Jennifer Grey Mystery Series

GATEWAY

*A
Jennifer Grey
Mystery*

Jerry B. Jenkins

Scripture Press

AMERSHAM-ON-THE-HILL, BUCKS HP6 6JQ
ENGLAND

© 1986 Jerry B. Jenkins

This book was first published in the United States by Moody
Press. Copyright 1986 by Jerry B. Jenkins

Scripture Press Foundation Edition printed by permission
of Moody Bible Institute, Chicago, Il.

First British edition 1990

ISBN 1 872059 17 1

Production and Printing in England for
SCRIPTURE PRESS FOUNDATION (UK) LTD
Raans Road, Amersham-on-the-Hill, Bucks HP6 6JQ by
Nuprint Ltd, 30b Station Road, Harpenden, Herts AL5 4SE.

1 Jennifer Grey and her fiancé, Jim Purcell, sat silently in the west parlour of the Norman Funeral Home on Chicago's Near North Side.

None but the macabre enjoy funeral homes. But those who have lost close loved ones develop a particular aversion to them. It can resurface and drag them back to wrenching memories at the mere smell of a sickeningly sweet floral shop years later.

Jennifer herself had been widowed young. So quickly, so painfully, that it had taken her months to regain a semblance of normality in her life. She had not been married a year when her husband was killed on the highway.

But she had dealt with that. Time, so the cliché goes, was a healer. So were close parents; understanding friends; a good church. And when she carefully ventured out into the real world again, Jennifer found she could function alone.

The loss made her reluctant to untie her emotions, hesitant to respond to her cautious new admirer. For a while she was able to hide, even from herself, her deepest feelings for Jim. Only sharing their own crisis and learning to depend upon each other had brought her to where she could no longer pretend she didn't care for him.

And now, after a long courtship, they would be married in a few months. She had said yes to Jim, resulting in the second to the last change in her life since her first husband's death. Until now, most of the changes had been for the better.

She had moved from the women's page of the *Chicago Day* to the newsroom under legendary city editor Leo Stanton. She and Jim had survived an ordeal in his career on the police force that, while it seemed to Jennifer almost as grieving as losing a partner, was really the beginning of their love relationship. She had been promoted to columnist with her own location on the front page.

Jim had only recently been promoted to sergeant and would soon be a plainclothes detective. Today he sat stiffly in his dress blues, wearing his funeral face, the one worn by all who were only loosely associated with the deceased.

Even Leo had been promoted. He had become managing editor just two months before. That meant a huge office on the sixth floor, a secretary, more business suits, less action, more headaches. He pretended not to like it, to be hemmed in, restricted from the fun of the daily grind, the hands-on editing.

But in truth Leo loved it. He deserved it. He had more policy input on the entire paper. Jennifer missed the measured casualness of dress that had characterized his reign of mock terror in the city room.

Leo had always been one for soft leather loafers or wing tips, grey woollen slacks, pastel shirts, navy or camel blazers, always draped neatly over a chair by mid-morning.

He liked to loosen his tie and roll up his sleeves, but there was still something formal about that informality. Worst, he had always felt the need to temper the whole look with a soggy, unlit cigar lodged in his right cheek.

He never smoked and frequently reminded everyone of that. Somehow, during the several weeks since he'd been promoted, he'd given up the cigar. Everyone guessed that publisher Max Cooper had made it a prerequisite.

Jennifer nodded red-eyed at her many colleagues as they sombrely stepped into the chapel. Mr. Cooper and his stately, white-haired wife sat near the front, behind the family. How strange not to hear his loud voice, his bellowing laughter. He had a reputation for bluster behind closed doors, but with the rank and file, he always seemed to feel required to joke and laugh and tell inane stories.

Jennifer turned to glance at Jim. His uniform made him look so young. The hat in his lap had left its telltale impression on his whitish-blond hair. His pale blue eyes noticed her looking up at him, and he pressed his lips together to acknowledge her.

The parlour was nearly full, though there was a line back to the lobby where many were still signing the guest book. Jennifer leaned to one side and peered up to the front row where the family sat, still stunned at their loss of just three days.

Leo sat in the middle of a nine-chair row, his left arm around his married daughter who sat next to her husband and their two young children. They had flown in the morning before from California. Leo's right arm was around his bachelor son from Maryland, who sat next to his mother's best friend — June Roloff — and her husband, Kent, assistant managing editor at the *Day*.

Someone had coached the grandchildren, who only occasionally looked at each other to whisper. Jennifer watched Leo for several minutes and wondered if he had even blinked. She didn't see him move.

He just stared straight ahead, not tightening his embrace on either his son or daughter, not looking at them, not speaking to them. It didn't appear he was crying. He simply sat with his arms around his family, like a statue.

Directly in front of him and about ten feet beyond lay the body of Samantha, his handsome, red-haired wife of thirty-seven years.

One of Jennifer's hands hid her eyes as she lowered her head and cried for Leo. Jim held her other hand in both of his. She had not known

what to say to Leo from the moment she had
heard of Samantha's death. She knew what not to
say, and from her too-fresh memories of just a
few years before, she decided her silent presence
was the best she had to offer.

Had it been over a month ago that she and Jim
had visited the Stantons' home? Jennifer had
been amazed at the beauty and charm of their old
West Town neighbourhood place, a narrow,
three-storey Georgian brick house they had lived
in since their marriage.

Jennifer had met Leo's wife at office functions,
of course, but she had never been to their home
until Samantha called one morning and asked if
she and Jim wanted to celebrate their engage-
ment over dinner.

Jennifer laughed at herself for being surprised
that Leo would even share such news with his
wife. He didn't seem the type, but then, certainly,
it was the type of thing a man would talk about
with his wife.

Samantha had been in her usual bubbly form
the morning she phoned. Her unusually low
voice and rumbling chortle were in fine fettle as
she joked about planning such an evening without Leo's knowledge.

'You wouldn't really, would you?' Jennifer
had asked, alarmed, making Samantha guffaw all
the more.

''Course not, dear. But it'd be fun, wouldn't it,
to see the look on that ol' bulldog's face when
company shows up for dinner? Ha! The biggest

surprise for him would be something decent to eat, know what I mean?'

Jennifer liked the woman immediately.

Their home was quaint and lovely, as one might expect when the wife is a world traveller and the man runs in fast company. Samantha was co-owner of a travel agency and taught a night school college course in oil painting.

At first Jim and Leo seemed a bit ill at ease with each other that night. Neither was a big sports fan, but each felt obliged to talk about different fixtures, under the assumption that the other wanted to.

When the ice was finally broken and they admitted that their real love was literature, they headed to Leo's study to discuss the editor's library. As they moseyed along the landing towards the book-lined cherrywood panelled den, Jennifer heard Leo tease, 'So how does a literate, non-sportsman wind up a cop, anyway?'

'He scream and holler at you a little now and then?' Samantha asked Jennifer after dinner.

'I was going to ask you the same thing,' Jennifer said, laughing.

'No, he doesn't,' Samantha had said, suddenly serious.

'I didn't think so.'

'Then why were you going to ask?'

'Because he screams and hollers a lot at the office. Yet here he seems so peaceful. And I like the way he's not afraid to hold your hand or put his arm around you in front of people. It's almost out of character for him.'

'I know what you mean, Jennifer. After all these years, too. I love it.'

'You're lucky.'

'Don't I know it,' Samantha said. And with a twinkle she added, 'And so is he.'

'Don't you two ever fight?'

'Nope. I do, but he doesn't. I'm the one with the Irish temper.'

'And he isn't?' Jennifer couldn't hide her incredulity.

Samantha smiled and tucked her feet up under her on the sofa. 'That's what so many of his employees say,' she said. 'You should have seen him with our kids.'

'Tough?'

'The opposite.'

Jennifer shook her head slowly.

'All his employees do that,' Samantha said. 'Nobody believes me.'

'Because you're having us on, or because he's so consistently on at us at the office?'

'Well, I'm not having you on,' she said. 'I think going on at his employees is just his way of drawing the best out of people. He drew the best from you, didn't he? You were on the society page or the women's page or something, weren't you? Now you're better known than he is.'

'Which is a little embarrassing for me,' Jennifer admitted.

'And which suits him just fine,' Samantha said.

The following week in the office, Jennifer had

chatted with Leo about Samantha. 'You don't talk about her that much,' she said.

'Sam? Nah, I guess not. Think about her all the time, though.'

'I wouldn't have believed that until I saw how you treated her the other night.'

'We get along.'

'You do better than get along. You enjoy each other.'

'Yeah, and after all these years.'

'That's what she said, Leo. Has it always been that good?'

'Mostly. Never any big problems. We disagree on politics, you know.'

'Really? She's not a conservative?'

'Anything but. Kids are the same. Drives me nuts. We don't talk about it much.'

'You have a super marriage,' Jennifer said.

'You sound surprised.'

'No, it's just that good marriages are so rare these days.'

'I know they are, but that's not why you're surprised. You think the only good marriages belong to you religious types.'

'Leo, you know religion has nothing to do with — '

'Yeah, yeah, all right. Born againers, then. Christians, evangelicals, whatever. You think they're the only ones with good anything. Good relationships. Good morals. Good marriages.'

'Not necessarily. They have bad relationships too.'

'Yeah, but they're the only ones with good marriages, am I right?'

'Apparently not,' Jennifer said.

'And you gotta admit that surprises you.'

'OK, maybe. But I'll tell you one thing: if your marriage is as good as it appears, I'll bet you're living under God's principles whether you know it or not.'

'How would we know? We're basically humanists. She more than I.'

'Let me guess. I'll bet you're faithful to her and always have been.'

Leo reddened. 'It's only fair. We promised each other that, and I know she's upheld her end of the bargain. That's why I do.'

'That's the only reason?'

He fidgeted. 'You know, I don't have to tell you — '

'I know, Leo, and I'm sorry. That was too forward.'

'That's OK, as long as you realize it. Another reason I'm faithful to her is because I love her, and I always have.'

'That's a biblical principle that works for you.'

'We aren't faithful because we think God wants us to be. We hardly believe in God. She doesn't at all.'

'But you do?'

'Sometimes. He fits my politics.'

'And I'll bet you don't go to sleep angry with each other.'

Leo looked at her, surprised. 'That's true,' he said slowly. 'How would you have guessed that?'

'Another biblical principle that makes for good marriages.'

'It's not because it's a biblical principle,' he said, growing louder. 'It's just that neither of us likes any tension hanging in the air, so we compete to see who can get the thing straightened out first. It works for us.'

'God doesn't require pure motives for His principles to work. They work no matter who uses them.'

'Lucky for us,' Leo said with an inflection that signalled the end of the conversation. Jennifer had felt more freedom in that discussion with him than ever before. She was glad she and Jim had visited their home. Maybe that had made it easier.

Four Fridays later, Jennifer had noticed Leo outside her glassed-in office visiting the newsroom. As a reporter said something that made him laugh, he was paged to the telephone.

Leo's face lost its colour and he hurried to a phone. Jennifer stood and moved to her door. Just as Leo slammed down the phone and ran to the lift, his face taut, she stepped out and grabbed Neil Scotto, the scurrying young reporter, on his way out.

'No time, Jenn,' he said. 'Got a possible death in West Town.'

She held his arm firmly. 'Is that what you told Leo?'

'Yeah!' he said, pulling away. 'I said it couldn't be him 'cause he was here. He said somethin' about nothing would surprise him in that neighbourhood any more. Jenn, I gotta go.'

'Where's your car, Neil?'

'At the back,' he called over his shoulder.

'Pick me up at the front,' she said. 'I'm coming with you.'

He looked annoyed, but she knew he'd pull around and wait for her. She gathered up her bag and threw her coat over her shoulder. On her way out through the lobby she paused just long enough to ask the receptionist, 'Who was that calling for Mr. Stanton?'

'A neighbour. Some kind of emergency.'

2 Jennifer had waited at the curb on Michigan Avenue for less than a minute when Neil screeched up and popped open the passenger door from the inside.

'Where you been?' Jennifer kidded him as the skinny, goateed reporter wheeled back into the traffic.

'Funny,' he said. 'I know we have to cater to you hotshot privileged columnist types, but what makes you want to ride along on a police call? Miss the old beat?'

'Sometimes. What's the call?'

'Lady saw her next-door neighbour's car in the garage later than usual. She wasn't worried. Thought she'd taken the day off. Wanted some company, gave her a call, no answer. Went over. Door was open, woman on her bed upstairs. Couldn't wake her.'

'Dead?'

'Who knows?'

'That's Leo's neighbourhood, you know.'

'Yeah, that's why I said somethin' to him. He laughed.'

'He's not laughing now. He got paged. The look on his face could have made me believe in premonitions, Neil. And after he took the call, he went past without even acknowledging me.'

'Doesn't have to mean anything, Jennifer. Not everyone bows before your altar on their way out of the city room.'

She ignored his crack. 'The receptionist said his call was from a neighbour. I don't like it.'

Neil fell silent. 'I don't either,' he said finally. 'We'll know soon enough.'

Jennifer was amazed at how different the neighbourhood looked in the daytime. The lawns seemed brighter, the alleys grimier, the houses smaller and closer together. Her mind raced as they neared Leo's home.

She began to speak, but Neil shushed her with a gesture. He was listening intently to the squawking from his police radio scanner when Jennifer heard the familiar address.

'Neil, that's Leo's house,' she said quickly. 'Is that where we're going?'

He nodded ominously, the humour gone. 'That's where we're going.'

Police had already cordoned off the house, and Neil had to park some distance away. Dozens of neighbours crowded the scene, pushing at the edges of the area.

An ambulance had backed into the Stanton driveway. Neil was still trying to talk his way past the police lines when Jennifer found Steve Jeski, an old cop she knew from her police beat days, and was escorted in the side door.

'So what's the deal, Steve?' she asked. 'I understand she didn't answer the door.'

'She's dead, Jenn,' the veteran said. 'Suicide.'

Jennifer wondered if she'd heard him right. 'Surely not,' she said. 'I knew this woman, Steve. No way.'

He motioned for her to follow. 'You ain't got a camera, right?'

She nodded.

He led her in through the kitchen, down the hall, and up one flight of stairs. Other officers leaned against the wall on the landing, giving Officer Jeski dirty looks as he and Jennifer picked their way through to the bedroom.

'Whadya need, Steve?' the officer in charge, a Lieutenant Theodore Crichton, asked as they approached the door.

'Just a peek,' he said, nodding at Jennifer.

Crichton recognized her. 'No pictures,' he said. They both nodded. Steve stepped back so Jennifer could peer in.

'Steve, she doesn't even look dead,' she said, without turning around. 'Are you sure?'

'She's dead all right, ma'am,' a paramedic said. 'Excuse me.'

He and his partner edged past her, wheeling a

trolley into the room. Samantha Stanton lay on her side on her bed. The bed had been made, and she was fully dressed and made up, including jewellery, as if for work.

It appeared she had perhaps stretched out to relax a moment. Her face was nestled in one hand and she looked peaceful.

Jennifer took a quick peek back over her shoulder at the officers huddling on the landing and leaned into the room. 'What was the cause of death?' she whispered.

'Self-inflicted poison,' a paramedic said.

'How do you know that?' she asked, insistently.

'They told us,' one said, pointing a thumb into the landing.

'*They* told *you*?' she asked. 'Aren't *you* supposed to tell *them*?'

The medic picked up Mrs. Stanton's bag and tossed it to Jennifer, who had the presence of mind to jump out of the way and let it fall to the floor. 'You shouldn't be touching anything in this room that you don't have to!' she scolded, nearly shouting. 'You may not know it, but this is a crime scene.'

'This is a suicide,' he said.

'Suicide is a crime too. Don't touch anything more! Didn't you even try to revive her?'

'Sure we did! Hey, who do you think you are anyway?'

'Shut up,' his partner said. 'She's a reporter.'

'Then get out,' the first said.

'I want to know how you could have tried to revive her in the position she's in.'

The police photographer entered. 'Everybody out,' he barked. Jennifer glared at the paramedics as she moved onto the landing. 'She back into the position you found her?' the photographer asked.

They nodded.

Jennifer stuck her head back in. 'You're shooting a re-created scene?'

'Who's askin'?'

'Jennifer Grey, *Chicago Day*,' she said.

'Talk to public relations downtown,' he said. 'I don't have to talk to you. In fact, I'm not s'posed to.'

'I just want to know if you're shooting the body the way it was found.'

'Yeah, sure.'

'How do you know?'

''Cause the paramedics got no reason to lie.'

'But they tried to revive her?'

''Course.'

'Not in that position they didn't.'

'Right again. You want a nice eight by ten glossy of this dame, or what?'

'So the paramedics worked on her and then put her back in the position they think they found her?'

'Somethin' wrong with that? Should they have waited till I got here for a few snapshots before they tried revivin' her, or what?'

'Leave 'im alone, Miss Grey,' Lieutenant Crichton said, touching her shoulder. 'He's just doing what he's told.'

'Your crime scene is being destroyed,' she said. 'One of the paramedics grabbed her bag with his bare hand.'

'We've already looked in her bag,' the lieutenant said. 'That's how we know it was suicide.'

'Your own men and the medics have contaminated the crime scene!'

'Nobody's contaminated nothin',' he said, pointing at the floor where the contents of Mrs. Stanton's bag had spilled.

Jennifer stared in disbelief at five booklets on suicide that had slid from Samantha's bag. She quickly scribbled their titles and publishers into her notebook as she heard commotion outside. Several officers bounded down the stairs to quell the disturbance. She moved to a window from which she could see Leo fighting to get into the house.

'Let me tell you something, Lieutenant,' she said, surprised at her own bravado. 'This woman's husband is managing editor of the *Day*, and he'll find a way in here soon enough. There'd better be no more messing up of this scene than there's already been, or a lot of people here are going to be in big trouble.'

Crichton screwed his face into a dirty look but stuffed the suicide booklets back into the bag himself. 'Jeski!' he hollered, putting the bag back next to the bed where it had been discovered. 'Get down there and tell them to let the husband in!'

He shooed the photographer and the paramedics from the room and pulled the door shut.

When Leo reached the top of the stairs, huffing and puffing, he saw Jennifer and the lieutenant and slowed to a stop.

Jennifer burst into tears at the sight of him, and the desperately angry look on his face melted into disbelief. 'Jenn?' he said pitifully, asking the question without saying the words.

She nodded.

'I want to see her.'

'You won't touch anything, sir?' the lieutenant asked.

He shook his head, and Crichton slowly opened the door. Leo knelt by the bed and impulsively felt Samantha's wrist for a heartbeat. He buried his face in her neck, and his sobs turned into a mournful, muffled wail that sliced through Jennifer like a winter wind.

She was tempted to make a deal with Lieutenant Crichton. The negotiation actually entered her mind, but she couldn't bring herself to broach the subject with him. It went against everything she believed in, and yet, in this case, she could have almost justified it.

She wanted to agree not to write about all the obvious errors in judgement and the sloppy evidence-gathering techniques during the last few minutes if he would agree to withhold from the other newspapers the discovery of the suicide booklets until the true cause of death had been determined.

But too many people already knew about the literature. Hiding it would be impossible — and unethical. Not writing about the shoddy police work would be wrong as well.

Her motive had been to protect Leo from embarrassment, she knew. Good motive, bad solution. She felt ashamed. The death *was* apparently a suicide. But how in the world would they ever know, the way the scene had been violated?

That night in Leo's home, she and Jim and Max Cooper and assistant managing editor Kent Roloff sat with the stunned widower and gently urged him to make funeral plans. He had spent much of the day on the phone to relatives, but he couldn't bring himself to talk about the cause of death.

'I don't know what we can do about it in the *Day*, Leo,' Roloff whined, tugging at his over-the-calf socks and twitching his narrow shoulders, as was his custom. He pushed his wire-rimmed glasses closer to his eyes with one finger and, in the same motion, dragged his hand back through his thinning hair.

He was wearing the threadbare grey plaid suit he wore nearly every other day, an ensemble that didn't seem befitting of a man who had enjoyed the same responsible and profitable position for more than a decade.

Max Cooper, ever in character, stood and pushed his pointed tongue out the edge of his mouth and swore. His white, bushy eyebrows set off the red face and jaunty, thick little body that always seemed ready for action. 'Of course you know what we can do about it, K.R.! It gets listed as a death of undetermined causes.'

Leo shook his head. 'That won't solve anything,' he said weakly, as if drained of life himself. 'Everybody knows that means suicide. Anyway, who's going to get the *Trib* or the *Times* to call it unknown causes?'

He buried his head in his hands and cried anew. By mid-evening the funeral arrangements had been set. 'Just family and close friends,' Leo repeated often. 'No press outside the *Day*.'

'That doesn't sound like you,' Roloff said, slapping Leo on the back.

'It does too,' he said flatly. 'I was never one for covering funerals, not even of gangsters. You know that. You tried to get me to cover enough of 'em. Made me cover a few.'

'Can't make you do anything now, can I?' Roloff said, smiling sympathetically.

Cooper swore again. 'You're unbelievable, Kent, you know that? You think it makes Leo feel good to be reminded that he's your boss now? That really makes everything all right, doesn't it? You ever stop to think that maybe your lack of tact is the reason you've been stuck in the same job for years?'

Roloff was embarrassed. 'I, I didn't mean anything, Mr. Cooper. I — '

'I know!' Cooper thundered. 'You never — '

'Hey,' Leo said, smiling and reaching out with both hands to the squabblers. 'Can you guys fight somewhere else?'

'I'm sorry, Leo,' Roloff said. Cooper stomped off.

'I want this thing covered in the *Day* the same way it'll be covered in the other two papers,' Leo said.

Cooper came back in an arguing mood. 'It's my paper,' he said. 'If I wanna protect my editor and his family, I can, can't I?'

'You can, Max, and I appreciate it,' Leo said. 'I really do. I don't believe Sam would have taken her own life any more than any of you do, I hope. In fact, I know better than any of you that she couldn't have. But if this happened to the wife of the editor of one of our competitors, I know we would cover it straight. We'd call it an apparent suicide, because that's what it is.'

'You believe that?' Jennifer asked.

'I believe it's apparent,' Leo said. 'I just know that what's apparent is not what is true. But there's only one way to cover it. The truth will come out eventually. My family and I will survive.'

Jennifer wasn't so sure. She pulled Mr. Cooper aside and told him she wanted to write the story in her column. He scowled and shook his head. 'I don't think so,' he said. 'I don't think Leo'd go for it.'

'I think he might,' she countered.

'Then *I* won't go for it,' he said. 'Clear?'

'Why?'

'I don't need to tell you why, young lady, but I will. Your coverage will impugn the police department, which may have to be done anyway.

But it will carry the bias of a personal friend and employee who doesn't believe what happened here any more than the grieving husband does. You're stunned. We're all stunned. Let the reporter — what's-his-name — handle it.'

'Neil.'

'Yeah, Scotto. It's the only way, Mrs. Grey. You're usually able to stay away from sentiment, but how could you here? It's not worth a column, outside of the fact that you work for the man and you knew them both. Am I right?'

Jennifer nodded, disappointed. 'Would you give me a short leave of absence?'

'For what?'

'To check this thing out. The coroner ruled it a suicide because of the books the police found and the poison he found in her system. The autopsy will find nothing else, and that'll be the end of it. You can't let Leo investigate it. He's not up to it, and he'll make himself miserable.'

'He's already asked for some time off himself. I hope it's so he can rest at his Wisconsin place.'

'Maybe if you told him I was going to check it out, he'd be able to rest. Otherwise he won't. When the shock wears off, if it ever does, he's going to want to get to the bottom of this. No matter what.'

'And what if you find that it *was* suicide, Mrs. Grey? We never know the private torment many people carry in their minds.'

'Then I'd have to think that would at least satisfy Leo. He'd want to know the truth, either way.'

3 The Saturday morning papers, all three major dailies, carried the stark story of the apparent suicide of the wife of a prominent editor.

The *Day* also carried a note that columnist Jennifer Grey would be on assignment for approximately two weeks.

In truth, she had been granted a leave of absence for not longer than three weeks.

Jennifer and Jim had invited Leo to church on Sunday, the day before the funeral, and he had almost accepted. 'Good strategy,' he had said wryly. 'Catch me at a vulnerable time.' But his family had flown in, and he would be at the funeral home all day.

Family, close friends, and no press except the *Day* turned out to be about 300 people. The Monday morning funeral became more of an ordeal than Leo expected. He had to be supported as he walked from the car to the grave site.

His older child, Mark, arranged to be away from his own business for a week and was set to go through his mother's things with Leo and then spend a few days at the Wisconsin cottage with him. Jennifer was glad Leo could get away and have company, but she wanted to talk to him first, if he was up to it.

Tuesday evening, when only Leo and Mark were in the house and Jim was on duty, she visited. Mark, a tall, brooding, darkly handsome man in his late twenties, sat in on the conversation but said nothing to Jennifer. He'd been away from home for many years, but it was apparent he knew his father.

Whenever Leo seemed to be losing control, when his breath came in short spurts and his lips quivered, Mark would change the subject or bring him something to drink. More than once, Jennifer got the impression that Mark felt she was intruding, that everything was happening too quickly, that his father needed time to himself to deal with his grief and put it behind him.

But Leo persuaded her otherwise. 'I need you to do this for me, Jenn,' he said, his voice breaking. 'I appreciate it more than you know. I wish I could help with strategy, but I can't think. You know what I mean.'

'Of course, Leo. You want to know where I'm going to start?'

He nodded.

'I've got copies of the literature that your wife had in her bag.'

'That was *planted* in her bag you mean,' he said quickly. 'That's the farthest thing from what Sam would have chosen to read, isn't it, Mark? Show her what your mother liked to read.'

Mark produced books on art and literature and, of course, geography and travel. Jennifer nodded and smiled.

'Still I feel it's important to know what those booklets are all about, don't you, Leo?'

He nodded again. 'I'd like to see 'em myself.'

Jennifer had them in her handbag, but she hesitated. Mark spoke up. 'No, you wouldn't, Dad,' he said firmly. 'Maybe some day. Not now.'

'Why not?'

'Trust me, Dad. Not now, all right?'

Leo smiled and clapped a hand on his son's thigh. 'All right, big guy. All right.'

Jennifer was relieved. She hadn't had a chance to read through them herself, but she knew they were nothing for a grieving man to see.

'I couldn't sleep in our bed,' Leo said suddenly, quietly.

'I can imagine,' Jennifer said, fighting tears herself.

'No, you can't, but thanks for saying so.'

'Leo,' she said, hoping the sound of her voice would remind him that she certainly *could* imagine, that she too had lost a spouse, that she could remember all too well the haunting emptiness of a bed that threatened to swallow her if she dared sleep in it alone. Even in his grief she couldn't permit him to pretend that he was the only one who had suffered this kind of grief, especially not in front of a fellow sufferer.

He looked up at her sadly. 'Jennifer, forgive me,' he said. 'I know you know. I remembered when you didn't try to say all the things everyone else tried to say.'

Mark glared down at her. She stood. 'I'd better go, Leo,' she said. 'I'll see you again whenever you say.'

'No!' he said, desperate and suddenly lucid. 'I want to know what you're going to do and how you're going to do it. I can't think clearly right now, but maybe if I know what you're up to, I'll think of something that'll help. Samantha didn't kill herself, Jennifer. You know that. And even if you don't, *I* do. If anybody can find the truth, you can.'

He was crying again. 'Leo,' she said, softly, 'you're not ready for this, are you? Let's talk again tomorrow, OK? I'll see you in the afternoon after I've talked to the coroner and the police and the woman next door.'

He nodded, his head in his hands.

Mark helped her with her coat and walked her to the front door. 'Thanks for being sensitive,' he said. 'You're very special to him.'

Jennifer was surprised. If anything, she had expected a lecture from the stern-faced son. In the light from the porch she could see that he was smiling a grateful smile at her. And he opened the door, gently guiding her through it with a hand on her arm.

He let his hand slide down into her gloved fingers, which he squeezed briefly while thanking her. 'We'll see you tomorrow,' he said.

Jennifer lay in bed till two in the morning reading the short booklets. They were as frightening and bizarre as anything she had ever read, not because they were horrifying or macabre. Rather because they were so reasoned, so deftly crafted, so persuasive.

The first made the clear point that the only prospect worse than an unacceptable life was a failed effort to terminate it. The book was the text for a euthanasia society that had nearly 10,000 members, all dedicated to the lofty ideal that they would rather take their own lives in relative peace and gentleness than to suffer a horrible end while enduring the ravages of disease.

The justification was on the basis of the reluctance of the dying to become burdens on their families or to suffer unduly themselves when the results would be the same regardless. They were going to die, so they wanted a hand in it.

Of course, the philosophy centred on the assumption that death was the total end of life. That's why the booklets, as genteel and slick as they were, stuck in Jennifer's craw. Because she believed that God was the author of life and that it was His to give or to take, euthanasia, regardless of the wrappings, was unacceptable.

Another booklet extolled the virtues of peaceful death, making it sound not only soothing, but desirable. Jennifer wondered what that might mean to those who weren't pain-wracked by disease or so old that they would rather be gone. She disagreed with suicide in any case, but making it so easy might tempt people who had even shallower reasons to consider it.

Everything she read pointed to suicide as an escape. There was no compulsion to face life head-on or to seek God or to serve others. One booklet referred to 'assisted suicide' as the 'compassionate crime'.

Assisted suicide, Jennifer thought. *I wonder what my homicide detective friends would call that?*

Another booklet presented the case for dual suicides and called self-inflicted death 'self-deliverance'. Jennifer shuddered. The language and the logic was not unlike what she had read in sales pitches for retirement villages in Florida.

One of the guides justified itself by hoping that it would aid in cutting down the incidences of botched suicide attempts. While making the case that suicide should be a last resort — at least a moderate approach compared to the others — it went on to prescribe specific doses of drug combinations that would result in deaths so peaceful that the body looks dead, but not disgusting.

Jennifer couldn't help but think of how Mrs. Stanton had looked on Friday morning. She would ask Jake Steinmetz, the Cook County Coroner, about the drugs found in the body.

Early the next morning, Jennifer visited the University of Chicago Law School library where she learned that in England it is a crime to aid a would-be suicide. In the U.S., she discovered, suicide, and even attempted suicide, are ironically punishable crimes and that assisting a suicide is also illegal.

She asked a law student, 'If it's illegal to aid a suicidal person in his effort, why can this material be printed and sold?'

'You ought to know that, if you're who I think you are,' he said. 'The First Amendment guarantees that you can write and publish anything you want. And so can the euthanasiasts. Don't threaten their freedom unless you're willing to have yours threatened as well. There are plenty of books available on how to lie, cheat, steal, and even murder.'

Jake Steinmetz was, as always, pleased to find a few moments for his favourite newspaper reporter. They had worked together many times in the past. He was shocked when she guessed the precise dosage of drugs found in Mrs. Stanton's system.

'Jennifer, I'm afraid I'm going to have to remind you that I am a friend of the court.'

'What do you mean by that?'

'Just that I'm sure that your boss has not been entirely ruled out as a suspect, and if you somehow know the dosage — well, that can't look terribly good for him. I would only be doing my duty to report it.'

'Jake, my boss would love nothing more than to think that this case was shifting in suspicion from a suicide to a homicide. Please tell me you'll do that, put him under suspicion, get them to admit that this could have been a murder.'

Steinmetz smiled his knowing smile. 'You set me up,' he said. 'All I was fishing for was how you knew the dosage. The cops aren't at liberty to release that yet.'

'I read it in a book, OK?'

'How did you know about the books?'

'I work hard, Jake. Just like you do. I do my homework. I have sources. Anyway, I was there.'

'I won't pursue that, Jennifer.'

'Thanks.'

'I'm satisfied it was a suicide.'

'Apparently for the same reason I'm convinced it wasn't,' she said.

'How's that?'

'Because the dosage matches the prescription in the book.'

'That's right.'

'Why not prove it?'

'We already know it, Jennifer. It's proven.'

'I mean prove the drugs were purchased by Mrs. Stanton. That should be easy enough. Wouldn't a pharmacist recall selling her lethal dosages?'

'No pharmacist in his right mind would fill a prescription like that.'

'Then where would she get it, assuming she got it?'

'Probably from two different pharmacies. The ingredients are not alarming in themselves. Only when mixed do they result in the deep, peaceful sleep.'

'That results in death.'

'Precisely.'

'That should be easy enough to check too,' Jennifer said. 'How many pharmacists are there in the area?'

'Hundreds. Be my guest.'

'I just might.'

'You probably will. That's what I admire about you, Jennifer. Naturally, if anything turns up, I'll be eager to hear about it.'

'Naturally. But you want me to do the leg-work.'

'Right again. As I said, I'm — '

'Satisfied. Yeah, I know. At least tell me how she ingested the dosage.'

'With water.'

'You're sure? It wasn't mixed with her food or dropped in her orange juice?'

'You're impugning your boss again, Jennifer.'

'I am not! Please stop saying that. If there's one thing I'm certain of, it's that Leo had nothing to do with his wife's death. I have to think someone poisoned her. If so, how would they have done it?'

'The autopsy showed a light breakfast and res-idue of an extremely fast dissolving mixture of the lethal chemicals, possibly in tablet form, but more likely mixed in water.'

'You're guessing.'

'Yes, I'm guessing she mixed it in water.'

'Why? To fit your suicide theory? Where are the prescription bottles? The spoon? The water glass? Would there not be residue on her water glass?'

'There was none. That's why I said possibly in tablet form.'

'You said it was more likely mixed in water. Why would she have been careful to clean the glass? Would she have had time?'

'Barely. She would have grown heavily drowsy almost immediately.'

'She took it in tablet form, Jake.'

'So?'

'One tablet she made up herself? No one would sell her that small a quantity of each ingredient, so where is the rest?'

'I don't know, Jennifer. This is your fairy tale, not mine.'

'Did you check any medicine bottles in her bag?'

'Of course, but this is totally off-the-record, Jennifer. No one has this. You can't print it yet.'

She raised her eyebrows. 'Deal,' she said.

'There was a bottle of plain, white aspirin tablets, the large type you take one at a time.'

'And?'

'Microscopic residue of the poisonous mixture on one of the tablets. Not enough to hurt a flea.'

Jennifer leaned forward in her chair. 'Jake! That means the death tablet could have been in that bottle, doesn't it?'

'What if it was?'

'Then it could have been planted!'

He shrugged and raised his hands in protest.

'Could have, could have,' he repeated, as if she were dreaming.

'There was no suicide note, Jake. How often does that occur?'

'I don't concern myself with suicide notes.'

'You never let a note help you determine a suicide?'

'Well, sure, I mean, sometimes it's obvious, and the note confirms it, and — '

'The woman was dressed for work, Jake. She had eaten a light breakfast. Don't you sometimes have to wonder why someone kills herself without a hint of the normal suicide pattern or even a reason?'

'Sometimes.'

'This time, Jake.'

'Happy hunting, Jennifer.'

4 'Are we off-the-record, Miss Grey?' Lieutenant Crichton asked, leaning back in his chair with his hands behind his head. She nodded. 'I've got to tell you I was on pins and needles all weekend waiting for your story to take us apart.'

'It could have.'

'Of course it could have. I'm fully aware of that. You were right. Why didn't you print what you saw?'

'I'm not on the story. Too close to it. Leo Stanton is my boss, and I knew his wife. The guy who's covering it, Neil Scotto, didn't see what I saw.'

'I'm glad, because we almost blew it.'

'Almost?' she said.

'You don't still think this was other than a suicide, do you?'

'I do.'

He shook his head slowly. 'Well, I feel some obligation to you for not making us look bad. We did a lot of things wrong, I'll admit that. But not publicly. I'm still convinced it was a suicide. But if there's any way I can help you, let me know.'

'Did you check it out, Lieutenant, or are you basing everything on what you found in her bag?'

'We checked her out some. You know, her interests and politics point to this sort of, ah, liberal, um, mercy-killing type of thing.'

'Euthanasia?'

'Right. She could have easily been into that.'

'But was she? Do you have any evidence that she belonged to any such group or was on any mailing list?'

He shook his head. 'That would require a lot of man hours, and the coroner is satisfied that it was suicide.'

'But how about pharmacies? Wouldn't it pay to find out where she got the ingredients?'

'We don't think so. I'm sorry. We just don't.'

'Yet you're willing to help me?'

'Sure, what can I offer?'

'Put Cap Duffy on this case.'

'Duffy? The homicide detective? I can't do that.'

'Why not?'

'First of all, I'm not in homicide. I can't go assigning their people. Second, if I *were* in homicide, I wouldn't put a homicide guy on a suicide.'

'Then what do you mean when you say you owe me, you're obligated to me, you want to help me? How can you do anything for me if you can't help me prove this wasn't a suicide?'

'You're gonna have to prove that on your own.'

'So you're not really willing to help me. You just appreciate that I didn't blow the whistle on your sloppy work at the scene of the crime.'

'At the scene of the death. When I offered to help you, I was thinking in terms of any driving or parking violations that you'd like me to investigate for you. Perhaps something I could check into more carefully than the arresting officer did.'

'Wonderful. You want to fix a ticket for me.'

'Oh, my — no, ma'am. I would never do something like that. However, I *do* have the power to interrupt the judicial process on certain violations if my investigation turns up mitigating circumstances, if you know what I mean.'

'I know what you mean. Fortunately, I don't speed, and the *Day* pays my parking tickets.'

'That *is* fortunate.'

'Yeah, for you too.'

'Me?'

'You just offered to fix a ticket. I could get you in big trouble.'

'I would never do anything of the sort. Maybe you have friends or relatives or acquaintances who might like to take their kids to the circus, but who can't afford it.'

Jennifer stood. 'Tell me you're kidding. You want to thank me for not writing the truth, which was hardly as a favour to you. And you want to show your appreciation by compounding the problem? No, sir! It's a wonder any crime gets solved in this city.'

Crichton smiled condescendingly. 'If I weren't still afraid you might point your poison pen at us, I'd warn you that a remark like that could result in your hoping you never *do* get a ticket in my precinct.'

Jennifer left without another word, more determined than ever to find out the truth on her own. She might seek Jim's counsel, but she couldn't involve him in the investigation.

Just after lunch she pulled into the driveway next to Leo's house. It appeared his car was gone. She hoped Mark had taken him out to lunch.

Mrs. Wilma Fritzee, Leo's neighbour to the south, was a lonely, talkative, sixty-five-year-old widow of nearly a decade who carried her age well. She fussed over Jennifer, bringing her tea and biscuits and leading a tour of the house.

'I know what it's like for Leo,' she said. 'The suddenness of it and everything. Edgar was older than I was, you know. Ten years. Retired from the foundry not three months. Died on our way to Florida for the big holiday we'd saved years for.'

'I'm sorry. I lost my first husband too.'

'Oh, my. And so young. But you're married again?'

'No, I shouldn't have said first husband. My only husband. I'm engaged.'

'How wonderful! I was almost engaged again myself, but I'm afraid my new man thought I had more money than I did. When he checked into that, he lost interest.'

'I'll bet you're glad of that.'

'Oh, in the long run I am. Who wants a man who marries for money? I always thought it was women who did that, but you know, I'd never do that. There are days, though, when I could go crazy without someone to talk to, and I wonder if the loneliness is worth it.'

'Worth the principle you mean?'

But Wilma Fritzee was lost in thought. Her eyes glazed over. 'Samantha was good to me,' she said. 'I can hardly believe she's gone. I would listen for her car leaving just before eight-thirty every morning, and I don't mind telling you I was always just a little disappointed when she left. She owns that company, you know, and she could pretty much come and go as she pleased.'

'And sometimes she didn't go to work?' Jennifer asked.

'Sometimes. Not very often. Usually she was out of there like clockwork. Leo — Mr. Stanton — he always left pretty early in that little car of his. 'Course he *never* misses work unless he's on his deathbed — oh, excuse me, I didn't mean to say it that way, but you know what I mean. Of course, you work for the man, so you know exactly what I mean.'

Jennifer nodded.

'But every once in a while, after Mrs. Stanton — Sam I always called her, it was all right with her — after she'd been on one of those one- or two-week trips to who knows where, she might be home a day or two the next week.'

'Resting from the trip?'

'Well, I guess so, but you know, it was never the first day or two after she got back because I guess she had to go into the office and get back on track or something. But after the trip and then after she'd been in the office a day or two, it would be like she wanted to wind down or take a break or something. That's when I would listen and hope I wouldn't hear that car of hers leaving the driveway.'

'And if it didn't?'

'I'd get right on the phone to her.'

'Weren't you afraid of disturbing her so early?'

'Oh, I'd look for the paper first. Leo, he leaves the morning paper for her because I imagine he gets one free at the office. If the paper was still out there, I'd leave her alone. But if it was gone, I'd know she's up. Know what? She usually was too.'

'Was what?'

'Up early, even on the days she took off. That's the kind of a woman she was. I loved her. Always have. Did anyway. It would make me so sad to think she really, you know, did it herself. I can't believe there could have been that much going on inside her head without me knowing about it.'

'You were that close?'

'We're the only two houses on this block that still have the same people in 'em for thirty years. We've been here since long before Leo and Sam moved in, honest. I remember when they moved in. Didn't even have kids then. Remember the kids bein' born, babysittin' 'em. Never had an argument all these years, though I used to get after those kids when they were little. But Sam didn't mind. She told me to holler at 'em if they were into somethin' they shouldn't be. What was your question?'

'I was just wondering if you were really close enough to know whether she was having some real difficulty, either physically or mentally.'

'I don't know. Maybe not. I know she just has tolerated me for the last several years since Ed's been gone. Not that we did much together as couples. Just a few cookouts each year, and Leo and Ed might sit out on the patio with a beer and watch a ball game on the portable.'

'Why do you think she was just tolerating you?'

'Well, because I was always the one to call her. She'd never call me first. And I don't blame her. Heaven knows I never gave her the chance. If her car was in and her paper gone by eight-thirty, ol' Wilma was on the blower. Never gave her much chance to even read the paper, I don't s'pose.'

'Did she ever make you feel like you were intruding?'

Mrs. Fritzee stood and moved towards the large picture window in her living room and leaned over the sofa to peer out past the shared driveway into the front garden of the Stanton home. She took a deep breath and let out a rattling sigh. Her voice was thick with emotion when she spoke again.

'No,' she said, straightening but not turning around. 'She never once made me feel anything less than a VIP. Her and Leo both. Treated Edgar the same way. We talked about that nearly every day of our married lives, I'll tell you that. Here was a foundry worker and a housewife. I never worked. Ed wouldn't have it. We suffered for it, but I wouldn't trade — '

Her voice trailed off as she remembered her other loss. But when she was ready, she picked up right where she had left off. 'Here was Leo, always a big shot with the newspapers. You know, before they started this new one you work for, there was five of 'em there for a while. Seems there was more than that years ago, maybe seven.

'But Leo was always right in the middle of one of 'em, bein' the number one guy in some section or another. Always movin' up. And Sam, she was makin' money from day one in that travel agency as soon as her kids was in high school; it had to been before Edgar died when she bought into the company. She's the only owner who works there, you know.'

'I didn't know that.'

'Oh, yeah. I think there's four other owners, something like that. But she owns half of it and runs it. I guess. I don't really know. That's sorta how it is. How it was, I mean. I don't know what happens now. Do you?'

Jennifer shook her head. Mrs. Fritzee seemed almost embarrassed, as if she suddenly realized that she was standing nearly in another room, forcing herself to talk loud enough for Jennifer to hear.

She shuffled back over and sat heavily, covered her mouth with an open palm, and let it slide down her chin. 'I was tellin' you what Ed and I used to say about them, wasn't I?'

Jennifer nodded.

'It was just that they always seemed to do good. Leo I'm sure was makin' OK money, and Sam did at least that good. They always had everything they needed and wanted, and they dressed well, travelled a lot, that type of thing.

'Edgar was a good worker, but there was never any money for him at the foundry. In forty-five years he worked up to quality control inspector and was shop union steward. We saved for that Florida trip for years and years, and the farthest we ever got away from here before that was a train ride to my sister's in New Mexico. We knew who we were and who we weren't, and we were happy, you understand.'

'I certainly do.'

'You have children, young lady?'

'No, ma'am.'

'That's good. I mean, that's good that they wasn't left without a father, you know what I mean? Only grief we ever had was our two boys. Neither one of 'em have amounted to much, but at least Edgar never really knew that. Both of 'em have kids their wives won't let 'em see. Pitiful.'

Jennifer silently agreed. Here was a lonely old woman with no-account sons who just lost the only apparent listener she had left in the world.

The old woman sighed again and seemed on the verge of tears. 'I keep gettin' off the track,' she said. 'The thing that Ed and I used to always say about Sam and Leo was that they treated us like friends.'

'Oh, I'm sure you *were* their friends, Mrs. Fritzee.'

'I know, but not really. I mean, we never went anywhere with them. We couldn't really talk about their lives. But Leo knew how to get Ed talkin' about the foundry, and Sam always told me about where she'd been as if next time I went anywhere, that's where it would be. I'm not kidding. She'd say stuff like, "You gotta watch it in the market there and make sure you get your best deal. Don't let 'em smooth talk you, Wilma," she'd say. And I'd laugh, 'cause there was no way I was goin' to wherever she was talkin' about, but it was fun to pretend.

'There's enough snooty people in this neighbourhood who got nothin' to be snooty about. And here was a couple who had every right to act above us all — because they was — and yet they was good as gold.'

She dabbed at her eyes with the end of her apron and stood again. 'Do you know,' she said, almost unable to speak, 'if either of us was ever in the garden when Leo or Sam had some big shot over, they would introduce us.'

'That's Leo,' Jennifer agreed.

'Both of 'em!' Mrs. Fritzee corrected. 'Sam too.'

Jennifer nodded. And the old woman wept.

5 By the time Jennifer was able to pull away from Mrs. Fritzee, Leo's car was back in his garage.

'Dad has had a rough morning,' Mark said, as Leo seemed to doze on the sofa. Jennifer could tell Leo was wide awake, but he lay there on his side in casual clothes and stocking feet with his eyes closed.

Jennifer was struck by how much he looked like his wife in her last repose, but of course she couldn't comment on it.

'How rough?' she whispered.

'He just wanted to go to a park they used to visit. We strolled around a while and then sat at their favourite picnic table. It wasn't easy for him. I hope it accomplished whatever he wanted it to. Strange though, I never went to that park before.'

51

'Why is that strange?'

'I just meant that it was apparently a place they had discovered after my sister and I had left home.'

'Wrong,' Leo mumbled, eyes still closed. Mark and Jennifer jumped. Mark smiled.

'Wrong?'

'Wrong. It was where we went alone, even when you two were around.'

'Hm. I feel left out.'

'That was the point.'

Mark laughed, apparently encouraged that his father's sense of humour was returning.

Leo sighed heavily and turned over, facing the back of the sofa. 'Shall we leave, Dad?' Mark asked.

Leo shook his head.

'Maybe talk in another room?' Mark suggested.

Leo shook his head again. 'I like you right where you are.' Soon he was breathing deeply, as if asleep.

'If he is, it's the first sound sleep he's got since Friday night,' Mark said.

Jennifer grimaced in sympathy, but Leo stirred, and she wondered if he could sleep soundly even now.

'I need to talk to my fiancé and make several other calls anyway,' she said. 'Perhaps I should come back later.'

'Oh, please stay,' Mark said. 'I enjoy your company.' His direct gaze made her uncomfortable, and she couldn't return it, though she was flattered. 'If Dad's not awake in an hour, I'll get him up with the smell of coffee and tuna fish, one of his favourite light meals. He hasn't eaten much.'

'You don't think you should let him sleep?'

'Oh, sure, if the smell of coffee doesn't wake him, I won't push it.'

'I needed to ask him about your mother's morning habits,' she whispered, 'and after talking to your neighbour, about the other partners in the travel agency too.'

'Well, I wouldn't know anything about the agency. I never took much of an interest in that, though I was proud of Mum for jumping into it. It made me want to start my own business. Which I did.'

'And which is?'

'Small sub-contracting firm. Plumbing and electrical. I know nothing of either one.' He smiled.

'I'll bet,' she said.

'Really! Well, just enough to keep my people honest. But my thing is business. I'd electrocute myself or drown if I started messing with the actual work.'

Jennifer almost laughed, but she saw the same look come to Mark's face that came to Mrs. Fritzee's when she realized she had joked about death when everyone's grief was so fresh. She changed the subject quickly.

'You don't recall anything about your mother's morning habits.'

'Not really. I suppose they're different now than they were when I was in high school. That was just before she started working. She was always a crack-of-dawn type. Up with Dad, breakfast for everybody but herself, then shooing us all out the door. Good mood in the morning. More than I can say for me or Dad.'

'She didn't eat breakfast?'

'Oh, yeah, but it was sort of her reward when she had everybody out the door. She'd settle at the dining room table with her newspaper and her toast and tea. And some kinda jam.'

'Marmalade,' Leo said.

With that, Mark stood and motioned for Jennifer to follow him to the kitchen. Leo grunted in protest when he realized they were leaving, but he stayed where he was and said nothing.

For half an hour or so, Mark and Jennifer sat across from each other at the kitchen table, chatting about everything except the Stantons. She told him about her husband, her home, her family, her job, and her fiancé.

Mark didn't appear to want to discuss Jim. Yes, he had met him at the funeral, but 'of course you realize I wasn't thinking rationally. I'm still not. I noticed *you* though; I do recall that.'

Jennifer didn't know what to say. 'So, your father likes tuna sandwiches? I don't think I ever knew that.'

'Only the way we make 'em here at home,' Mark said, rising and expertly preparing a pot of coffee. He noticed Jennifer's surprise. 'From years of living alone,' he said. And she looked away.

He popped a can of tuna into the electric opener as if he'd done it every day of his life, picked the meat from the can with a fork and got every morsel, and mixed it in a plastic bowl with plenty of mayonnaise. Then he added diced onion, sweet and dill pickle, and celery.

'You like olives?' he asked, suddenly looking up.

She smiled and shook her head. 'Not in tuna,' she said.

'Great,' he said. 'I was looking for a reason for us to drive to the supermarket.'

'You shouldn't leave Leo right now anyway, should you?' she asked, wishing she'd been bolder and just told him to back off. She was, after all, engaged, not available, not interested. Well, at least two out of three.

'I s'pose not,' he said, rummaging around for a platter for the sandwiches and a bowl for crisps. 'You want Coke, milk, tea?'

'Coffee is fine,' she said.

He placed everything in the middle of the kitchen table, and as if on cue, his father padded in from the living room. Noticing the table, Leo couldn't suppress a sad smile. 'Always said you'd make somebody a fine wife some day.'

Mark shook his head in mock frustration. 'Sit down, you old coot.'

Mark was pouring the coffee when his father surprised him. 'I want Jennifer to say grace,' he said, more as an announcement than as a request. 'You mind, Mark?'

His son was taken aback, but he just shrugged.

'Jennifer, would you?' Leo asked.

'Sure,' she said, panicking. Wasn't it Leo who

had advised her to stop praying over her meals at the office and with her colleagues? She had never prayed aloud, of course, but she had always felt she should just bow her head.

She had told Leo she didn't feel she was making a show of it, and he told her it made everyone uncomfortable. She asked a few friends, who agreed with Leo and who added that it seemed a little holier-than-thou.

She had even talked it over with her parents, who thought she should continue it as a witness. 'You never know who might be affected by that little gesture,' her father said.

But she had decided to stop doing it. She wasn't doing it for a witness, and she certainly didn't want to make a show of it, which was hard to avoid because people noticed, no matter how subtle she was.

It had been months since their discussion, and she had felt a little guilty about opting out. But she had got over that. She and Jim prayed together, of course, and even at meals. And she prayed during her own time alone.

But now Leo wanted her to pray, aloud and in front of his son — a self-proclaimed humanist, basically agnostic, almost atheist — and himself, a basically patriotic right-winger whose god was conservative politics and the free enterprise system.

She bowed her head and closed her eyes, her heart drumming. 'Father God,' she began, 'thank you for your love and for your provision of food. Thank you for a family of people who care for each other. Be with them in their time of grief. In the name of Jesus Christ, Amen.'

There was a moment of awkward silence before Leo reached for a sandwich. Though he didn't speak, it was obvious he was overcome with emotion. He fought tears and chewed slowly, as if not really hungry.

Mark ate quickly, nervously.

'Delicious,' Jennifer said.

'Yeah, Mark. It's good,' Leo said.

Mark nodded. He had stopped staring into Jennifer's eyes, as he had done all afternoon. She decided that if her prayer had had no other effect than to put him off a little, that would be fine. And then, of course, she felt guilty for that.

Except for those brief compliments to the chef, they sat in silence. After a few minutes, less than half a sandwich, and one cup of coffee, Leo rose unsteadily and apologized.

He shuffled from the room with the fingers of his right hand pressed to his forehead. He peeked under his hand to see where to walk. Jennifer and Mark stood quickly and watched him amble back to the sofa where he sat and cried, his head in his hands.

Suddenly, Jennifer wasn't hungry. Mark encouraged her to finish, but she couldn't. He wolfed another half sandwich and took his cup with him into the living room. Jennifer followed.

'Enough action for one day, Dad?' Mark said smiling. 'Shall I kick her out or take her somewhere?'

Leo wiped his eyes and tried to force a smile.
'I'd rather kick you out and let her stay,' he said.

'This may not be the right thing to say, Leo,'
she said, 'but it hurts me to see you hurt.'

'I appreciate that,' he managed. 'I'm all right.'
He winked at Mark. 'It's just that his mother
made those sandwiches so much better than he
can!'

'Ouch!' Mark said. 'I thought they were particularly good.'

'So did I,' Jennifer said.

And the awkward silence returned. The sun
was setting, and Mark stood to close the curtains.
'Leave them open, if you don't mind,' Leo said.
He sat with his hands in his lap, his shoulders
sagging, staring out into the twilight.

'You haven't seen me like this, have you,
Jenn?' he said.

She shook her head, not able to speak.

'Big tough guy editor, never needs anything or
anybody, right? That's me. I can hassle everybody, afraid of nobody. I'm champion of the old-
fashioned cause. We do it right because that's the
only way to do it. Credibility and trustworthiness
and our reputation is all we have, right?'

Jennifer didn't know what he was driving at,
but she nodded. It reminded her of his late-night
harangues against sloppy journalism or management selling editorial out for the sake of an
advertising dollar.

Leo would fight with anybody, even Max
Cooper, over principle. And Leo usually won.

'But the only reason I could do that without

fear,' he was saying now, 'is that I came home to the Rock of Gibraltar.' His face contorted, and the tears flowed, but he made no move to hide them or wipe them away.

Jennifer impulsively sat next to him and put her arm around his shoulders. He sobbed.

She peeked at her watch. She would meet Jim in an hour, but she needed information from Leo first. She wanted to be clear on his wife's morning routine. She wanted to know of the other partners in the travel agency. And she wanted to know what pharmacies the family used. But she didn't dare ask.

She tried another tack. 'When are you heading for your cottage, Leo?'

He shrugged. 'The sooner the better, I guess. Do you think I'm weak, Jennifer?'

'Leo, you're one of the strongest men I've ever known. You've meant more to me in my career than anyone. You're hurting and grieving, and you shouldn't fight that. Let it happen. If you weren't tender right now, after a long and good marriage to a wonderful woman, I'd worry about you.'

He nodded. 'I'm not going to sleep tonight. I just know it. And I need to. I'm exhausted.'

'You must be,' she said. 'Do you ever use sleeping pills?'

'Never have,' he said, 'but right now I'd be willing to try.'

'Where would you get them?' she asked.

'I'd want a prescription,' he said. 'None of these over-the-counter things.'

'I can call your doctor, Dad,' Mark said. 'You still see Billings?'

Leo nodded.

'What pharmacy do you use, Leo?' Jennifer asked as Mark went to the phone.

He thought a moment. 'Hargreaves on Western,' he said. 'Or the one next to the grocery store on Kedzie.'

When Mark returned, he told his father that Dr. Billings had advised against sleeping pills. 'He said he'd be glad to prescribe valium — '

'No way!' Leo said, almost shouting. 'I've read enough about that to know I wouldn't touch it. Forget it. I'll just ride this out.'

'He also said that in case you were still as belligerent about valium as you were the last time he saw you — which, he wanted me to remind you, was more than eighteen months ago — a change of scenery might be the best medicine.'

'You tell him we were going up to the cottage tomorrow?'

'Yeah. He said make it tonight.'

'Tonight?'

'Tonight. He said you'd probably sleep in the car on the way up there, which would be good, even if you didn't sleep well once you got there.'

'If I'm sleepin' when we get there, leave me in the car. When do we leave?'

Leo had so brightened at the prospect of the trip that Jennifer knew she could ask him what she needed to. 'Why doesn't Mark pack a bag for you while you chat with me,' she suggested. 'Just give me enough to keep me going on this until you get back.'

6 Leo painfully told Jennifer the mundane details of his wife's morning routine. For some reason he found it particularly difficult. Just thinking about her in her normal habits of life seemed almost too much for him.

Several times Jennifer offered to put it off till another time, but Leo wouldn't hear of it. 'In the middle of this pain, I feel more strongly than ever the need to prove she didn't kill herself, Jennifer.'

He told her his wife rose with him, made their breakfast, and just before her last cup of tea, she would finish dressing and making herself up for work. Then she would clear away the dishes, run upstairs for a final shot of mouth wash and some lipstick and peek in the mirror, and then head back downstairs to read her paper until it was time to leave.

The phone rang. It was Kent Roloff's wife. 'Yeah, June, how ya doin'?' Leo asked. 'Oh, I'm OK, thanks. It's not easy, June.... Yes, I know, it's hard on all of us. You were close, yes.... Twenty years? I wouldn't have guessed it was that long.... Well, I don't believe it either, but I'm working on that.... Yeah, Mark's running me up to the cottage for a few days.... Right, last summer.... Uh-huh, that was fun. Maybe we can do it again this year. You two and me anyway, I mean.... Oh, I'm sure Kent is taking care of everything for me. Tell him I appreciate it, if I don't get to talk with him.... Oh, he is? Well, all right.... Hi, Kent.... Yeah, I hope to see you next Monday.... No, I won't rush it. I'll let you know. Thanks for everything, buddy.'

Leo hung up and rolled his eyes. 'If the truth were known, I can hardly stomach the man,' he said. 'June's a doll, though. Always fun to be with. She and Sam were like sisters. This is as hard on June as it is on me.'

'Surely not.'

'Well, she thinks so. I don't think she has any idea. But they *were* close. June helped Sam in her travel class. She took the course and then served as sort of a volunteer aide. Did that for years. Could probably teach the course herself by now. And when Samantha won trips for two and I couldn't go, which was at least once a year and sometimes two, June was always her first and only choice. Their friendship was developed around the world.'

'She never took Mrs. Fritzee?'

'You know, she asked her once. June couldn't go for some reason, and Sam plucked up her courage and asked Wilma.'

'Why did that take courage?'

'You've talked to the woman. Sam was afraid she'd talk all the way to Bangkok and back. Probably would have, too.'

'Why didn't she go?'

'Didn't have a dime for clothes or souvenirs or incidentals, and Sam didn't want to offend her by offering to give her cash too, though she would have been happy to pay for the companionship. Sam was really quite relieved when Wilma said no. She wound up taking one of the gals from the office.'

'Do you feel up to telling me about her business, Leo?'

'Yeah. She owned half of it, and there are four other shares at twelve and a half per cent each.'

'Who owns them?'

'I hardly know. One's an investment banker who just sees it as a good investment. There's a retired couple in Texas who own a piece. And then there's a holding company of some kind — it's got initials in its name — that owns the two other shares.'

'Is it worth checking into, Leo?'

'What — the ownership? Aw, I doubt it. They're mostly friendly. They have semi-annual meetings where the couple from Texas, the banker from downtown, and a local lawyer representing the holding company meet with Samantha. Guess I'll have to get involved in all that baloney now. She left me forty per cent of the company.'

'Only forty? That means you still have controlling stock by quite a significant margin. But if that holding company buys one of the other small shares out, you'd only have a small edge on them.'

'Good grief, Jennifer, I could hardly care less. I'd be happy to sell it out to them myself.'

'Do you mind telling me who your wife left her other ten per cent of the company to?'

'Not at all — it was a wonderful gesture. Just a little nest egg for June Roloff.'

'That was a nice thought, Leo. But do you see how it threatens your control of the company?'

'I suppose, but I'd always have June in my corner, so there's no way anyone can get more than fifty per cent. In that sense, it's just like it's always been. I'll wind up splitting my shares between my kids some day anyway. Problem is — unless I sell, which I really shouldn't — I have to be chairman of that stupid board. Major stockholder gets that dubious honour. It made sense when Sam was the owner. They pretty much liked having the chairman of the board running the company because she had more at stake than any of them. They had to know she'd run it for profit.'

Jennifer had the uneasy feeling that she should check into the ownership a little more thoroughly. 'I know you think it's a dead end, Leo, but is there a file or anything I can see that would give me a little more on the agency?'

'It might be at her office; it might be in her desk in the den upstairs. If the permission is mine to give, you have it. I'm not sure it's all legally mine yet until it goes through litigation, so you might have trouble getting into the files at her office. Check the den; be my guest.'

Mark came down with two suitcases and carried them out to the car. 'I'd really like to look through her papers, Leo, but I don't want to hold you up.'

'Nonsense, you won't hold me up. Just lock up when you're through. The lights are on timers. You might let Mrs. Fritzee know so she doesn't call the cops.' He embraced her briefly and gently and thanked her for listening and understanding.

'Just take care of yourself,' she said. 'I'm not goin' back to work until you do.'

Mark winked at her, but she pretended not to notice. After calling Mrs. Fritzee, Jennifer phoned Jim to tell him she would be a little late. 'But I still need to talk to you tonight,' she said. 'Nine o'clock too late?'

'Are you kidding? Any time, any where, kid.'

She laughed. 'The Pancake House on Western.'

'Pretty late breakfast,' he said. 'See you then.'

Jennifer had always been fascinated by personal papers. She would rather nose around in someone's desk than in their wardrobe or even in their safe.

It didn't take her long to determine that Samantha Stanton kept excellent records, and while most of the day-to-day business papers

67

were apparently kept at the office, what Jennifer really needed was right there.

In a file labelled 'Board', Jennifer found the minutes of the semi-annual meetings of the stockholders of the Gateway Travel Agency. Most were mundane financial reports and guest appearances by various staff members, reporting to the stock holders on different aspects of the company.

Jennifer traced the history of the company from the time Mrs. Stanton bought in and became the major stockholder. The technology and the relationships with airlines were the most dramatic differences, with Samantha campaigning for total computerization of the operation.

Most interesting, she found that the two most vocal members of the board were Kimberly Rand, the wife half of the Texas couple — Mr. and Mrs. T. J. Rand — and a lawyer named Conrad Dennison, who represented the holding company K.R.C. Limited.

The investment banker, Wilfred Griffin, seemed a positive man from the minutes, always the first to express appreciation ('I'm sure on behalf of the entire board — ') for anything and everything presented.

Mr. Rand always backed up his wife, but rarely led any dissent. Dennison was the troublemaker, frequently asking tough, accusatory questions and debating the majority on almost every vote.

On three separate occasions, Dennison tendered cash offers for the stock of both the Rands and Griffin in the middle of a business meeting.

On two other occasions, official complaints were noted in the minutes — once by the Rands and once by Samantha Stanton herself — citing the lack of proper procedure in tender offers he had made between meetings.

Chairman: "Let the minutes show that the representative for K.R.C. Ltd. made an improper offer to purchase 60 per cent of my stock or 30 per cent of the company, tendering his offer by phone and without proper documentation."

K.R.C.: "What's the purpose of putting that in the minutes? I have every right to make a bid for a total majority, and you have every right to refuse it. It appears here as if I've broken some law."

Chairman: "If you need the reminder, our bylaws call for the knowledge of the entire body notified by mail before any such transaction is undertaken. And for the record, my stock is not for sale at any price."

K.R.C.: "We'll see. I just wonder how profitably this company could be run with proper majority control."

Griffin: "I feel very good about how the company is being run. We survived the recession with just one losing quarter, and we've been very profitable for many years."

K.R.C.: "Perhaps our ideas of profits differ, Mr. Griffin. This company is mostly

a liability to my clients, almost a tax write-
off. It could be twice as profitable."

Jennifer wanted to meet the Conrad Dennison
character representing K.R.C. She also wondered
who was behind K.R.C. If, by any chance, it was
connected with anyone already owning one of
the smaller shares, the purchase of the remaining
small share would put half the stock in their
hands. Then the *real* battle would begin.

The addresses and phone numbers were all
there, so Jennifer took as many notes as she could
and tried to keep it all straight in her head. Just as
she was about to put everything back where she
found it, she noticed a pile of unopened mail.

Much of it consisted of bills and junk mail
addressed to Leo. But a few pieces were for
Samantha. Apparently, Leo had dumped everything on her desk that wasn't obviously a sympathy card.

At the bottom of the stack was an unopened
six by nine manila envelope from K.R.C. Ltd.,
addressed to Samantha over her agency title. Leo
had said to be his guest. Did that permit her to
open his mail? His wife's mail? Would she be
violating the law — opening a dead woman's
mail? The woman's heir had given her permission, sort of.

This was agency business. Leo would be inher-
iting majority stock. Did that give him total right
to this envelope? And if so, had he given Jennifer
the right to open it?

It was much too early to call Wisconsin and get

Leo's permission. What about the *Day* lawyer who had represented Jennifer a couple of times? No, he would want to know who she was talking about, and he would advise against it.

He would advise against it, she knew, because it was wrong. Maybe Jim would know if there was any way she could justify it. She dialled. No answer at his apartment. She called his precinct station house. No, he had already left for the day.

Jennifer looked at her watch. It was almost time to leave if she was going to meet Jim at nine o'clock. She held the envelope up to the light. Nothing. Too thick. She studied the outside carefully.

It had been typed in legal typeface, and the name Dennison had been added, also typewritten, above the return address logo. K.R.C. Ltd. had an Evanston post office box, but the office address was on North Sheridan Road in Chicago.

Was it a firm in its own right, or was it simply represented by Conrad Dennison's law firm? How could she know? How could she find out?

Curiosity was killing her. The postmark was the previous week. It must have arrived Friday or Saturday. No earlier, or Mrs. Stanton would have opened it.

What if it was a proper legal offer, a copy of which was sent to all the other stockholders? Shouldn't Leo be made aware of it? But then, nothing could be transacted until Samantha's will was executed, right? Leo'd be protected.

But what if an offer was being made on another minority stockholder, and Leo wanted to match

71

or beat the offer? If they didn't hear from Leo by a certain time, the deal would be consummated. Then what?

And what if Jennifer was right about K.R.C. representing someone else on the board? Leo could get back into his daily routine, show up at his first board meeting, and find he was majority stockholder with just forty shares to K.R.C.'s thirty-seven and a half.

All of a sudden the bidding for the remaining two shares — June Roloff's ten per cent and the unsold twelve per-center — would become fierce. Leo should be aware, shouldn't he? Wasn't it Jennifer's duty to her boss and friend?

She knew it was not.

Twenty minutes later Jennifer was pouring out the story to Jim in the parking area of the Pancake House. He tried to slow her and quieten her down as they entered and found a table, but she was going on and on about her dilemma.

He smiled, just listening to her. She sped through the information she had read in the minutes and dwelt on the curious envelope, the one she just didn't think she could resist. It drew her like a magnet.

'I worked like anything to talk myself out of opening it,' she said.

He nodded. 'Good.'

'And then I tried everything to talk myself *into* opening it.'

He stopped nodding. 'You didn't.'

She dug in her bag and produced the envelope.

'I hoped it would have one of those gummy flaps that could be pulled apart and then resealed.'

'But it didn't?'

'No.'

'That's good, because that wouldn't have made it any more right or wrong to do.'

'But, Jim, you should see what it says.'

His eyes fell. 'You didn't.'

She held it up to his face. The envelope had been slit. 'Just wait till you hear what it's all about.'

7 'Just water, please,' Jim told the waitress
evenly. 'I'm not eating.'
'I am!' Jennifer said. 'I'm famished.
Give me the blueberry pancakes and the
works.'

'The works?'

'Whatever comes with it — everything. Hash
browns, toast, milk, orange juice — whatever.'

'Only syrup and whipped cream comes with
it, ma'am.'

'Fine.'

Jim was stony. His eyes appeared hooded, and
he sat with his chin in his hand, staring at her,
expressionless, as she recounted what she'd
found in the envelope. 'I'm not sure I want to be
party to this,' he said at one point.

'You don't have to be,' she said. 'I know I'm in

this alone. But Leo won't mind. Believe me — I know him.'

'He may forgive you, Jenn. But it was still wrong to do it without asking first.'

'I couldn't reach him! And I couldn't wait. I was right. It's important, and he needs to know about it.'

Jim shrugged, and Jennifer sensed frustration building inside her. He was coming off a little pious in this, as if he and the rest of the police didn't go snooping when they felt like it. 'You want to hear this or not?' she asked.

He didn't respond, which embarrassed her. So she began without looking at him. 'You see, it's notification to all stockholders that K.R.C. Ltd. is making an official offer to buy out Mr. Griffin's twelve and a half per cent. He's the investment banker with one of the small shares.

'The way it works in this kind of company is that the offer does not have to be matched or even accepted. But if it *is* accepted, or if there is an indication that it will be accepted, other stockholders may tender private bids of their own, without knowing the original bid.'

She waited to see if Jim had any questions. He remained in the same posture, staring at her as if disappointed. He *was* disappointed. He had already made that clear.

'So,' she concluded, 'K.R.C. has notified the seller and the other stockholders of its intention. If the buyer doesn't hear anything by Friday of this week, the offer will be official. Now this Griffin has always been happy with his invest-

ment, but with the death of the principal stockholder, he may accept a good price. He's no fool,
and he has not been really active in the decisions
of the company. He's just gone along with everything Mrs. Stanton wanted to do.'

Jim would not participate in the discussion.

'Don't you think Griffin might want to get out,'
she pressed, 'knowing that Mr. Stanton has no
interest in running the business and also knowing that K.R.C. will undoubtedly take over the
majority stock eventually?'

No response.

Jennifer ate, occasionally glancing up to see
Jim staring at her, still unsmiling. She smiled at
him. He looked away. She'd rather he told her off
than put her off like this. She lost her appetite
quickly.

'OK, all right,' she said. 'I think you've carried
this judgement far enough. I was wrong. I admit
it. I'm frankly glad I did it, though, because I
think Leo will want to know. All right? Are you
going to hate me for ever because I didn't live up
to your ideal of me?'

Jim just sat looking at her, letting the words
echo in her mind so she could hear herself. She
only felt worse.

'Do you realize,' he said finally, 'that you're
sidetracked from your mission?'

She looked puzzled.

'Your job is to prove that your boss's wife
didn't commit suicide. Based on what was found
in her body, it was either suicide or murder.
Couldn't have been an accident. How has this

mail you've tampered with helped you determine her murderer?'

Jennifer sat back and sighed. She was still upset at Jim's condescending attitude, but she wished she had an answer for that one. All of a sudden she was running the travel agency instead of protecting Samantha Stanton's reputation.

'Jennifer, you have to tell Leo what you've done. You can't let it go long. These things have a way of catching up with us.'

Now she was furious. 'All right, Jim, I'll call Leo now! Is this thing so serious with you that it harms your view of me?'

'Why put the blame on me? It was wrong, and we both know it. You're entitled to mistakes; that doesn't shatter me. But I *do* wish you'd stop trying to justify it and would just deal with it!'

She stomped off to the pay phone, knowing Jim was right, wishing he wasn't, and mad at herself for going against her own conscience. She also wondered what Leo would say.

'He's sleeping, Jennifer,' Mark said. 'And guess where?'

'Not in the car.'

'In the car. And I mean he's out like a light. The weather's nice, and the car's right next to my bedroom window, so I can keep an eye on him. I'm gonna let him sleep. I'm glad you called though. Dad got all worked up when he remembered that some letter was still on the desk from one of the company stockholders.'

'That's what I was calling about.'

'Good. He called the lawyer at the newspaper and the guy agreed to represent Dad in the agency, help him hire someone to take it over, and all that. He said to just leave that envelope unopened, because if it's any kind of official business, it'll be null and void or something like that as soon as the lawyer points out that it arrived during the week of my mother's death. OK?'

'That's the problem, Mark. I opened it.'

'You opened it? Why would you open it?'

'I thought it might be something important. And it was.'

There was silence on the other end for several seconds. 'Oh, boy,' Mark said finally. 'Dad's not going to like that. Neither will his lawyer.'

'I was trying to help.'

'By opening his mail? I'm not sure how that helps, Jennifer.'

'Me either,' she muttered.

'Pardon me?'

'Listen, Mark, since what's done is done, you'd better get the message to the lawyer so he can do something about it.'

'What's done is done? That's your view of it?'

Jennifer sighed and rolled her eyes. *Not from this guy too!*

'I'm sorry. I shouldn't have. I tried to reach you, but it was too early.'

'We tried to reach you just before nine,' he said.

'I was gone already. Are you going to chastise me for it, or are you going to tell the lawyer?'

'I'll tell him,' he said. 'But I think I'll let you tell Dad. You owe me that, at least.'

'I *owe* you?'

'*I* didn't open his mail.'

Jennifer reminded herself that Mark was grieving. Maybe if nothing else came of this, his interest in her would wane. That would almost make it worth it. Problem was, she feared the same was happening to Jim. Maybe he'd back off if he knew she knew he was right. And if he knew his prediction was right. It had indeed caught up with her.

She trudged back to the table and told Jim. He reached across the table and took her hand. 'I was a little rough on you, and I shouldn't have been.'

'Of course you should have,' she said. '*I'm* even disappointed in me. I could have helped more by leaving it alone. They would have beaten it by not opening it. Now they have to go on the offensive. And like you said, it's totally off the subject of her death.'

'Totally?'

Jennifer shot him a double take. 'What are you saying?'

'Think, Jenn. You didn't get into that desk to look for some partner buying another partner out, did you? Didn't you have a reason you wanted to know more about that business? Wasn't it related to your original purpose here?'

'Yes, I was looking for a murderer.'

'Of course. That might sound a little silly now, but you can't leave any stone unturned. It was a hunch, and you played it. What did you expect to find?'

'Some irregularity, some enemy, some reason someone might benefit from Samantha Stanton's death.'

'And did you find it?'

'I'm not sure.'

'But you've got plenty to go on, lots to check out before you pull out from under this rock, am I right?'

'You're right. When do you become a detective, Sweetheart?'

'Not soon enough.'

'Tonight, I think. Thanks. Now aren't you hungry?'

'As a matter of fact, I am. You got time to watch me eat?'

'Depends. What are you ordering?'

'Just what you did.'

'Want what's left of mine?'

'Oh, sure. Cold pancakes are one of my favourites.'

The next morning she called Jim before heading out to talk to the two pharmacists on her list. 'I saw you angry with me last night.'

'For the first time?' he asked.

'You tell me. Have there been other times?'

'I dunno.'

'You do! I can tell from your voice! When?'

'I don't remember.'

'You do — '

'No, I really don't. I just know it hasn't been

the first time, that's all. Maybe a long time ago. Last night I just decided to let you know it, that's all.'

'That one of your philosophies? If it's important enough, you'll tell me, and if it isn't, you'll let it slide?'

'I guess so.'

'Is that good?' she asked.

'I think so.'

'So do I. Any more thoughts before I go out and play detective today, Sergeant Purcell?'

'Uh, what are you expecting from the pharmacists today, Jenn? They're a pretty tight-lipped bunch unless you have a warrant or something.'

'I know. But apparently there was nothing wrong with the two isolated ingredients she might have got at different times.'

'Still, they're prescription drugs, so there would have to be a record.'

'Of course, my theory is that there will be no record whatever of her purchasing the ingredients.'

'I thought of another obstacle you should be aware of. Maybe you already know.'

'Go ahead. I need whatever I can get.'

'It's just that Mrs. Stanton's philosophy and politics are not in your favour. The minister, or whatever he was, did a good job avoiding the suicide angle at the funeral, but the fact is, she might have been comfortable discussing just those ways to die. Not that she would have. Nothing in her history or personality indicates that she would have chosen it for herself, but can't you see her arguing for euthanasia under the right circumstances?'

'I guess so, but unless she had some terminal illness, which the coroner didn't find — either that, or Jake's not saying — she certainly wouldn't have been preoccupied with it from the perspective of her own life.'

'I agree. Just something to think about.'

'Anything else?' she said.

'Yeah, as a matter of fact. Just before we left last night, you recounted Mrs. Stanton's morning routine. Did you come to any conclusions based on that?'

Jennifer thought a moment. 'Well, yeah,' she said. 'I guess I just thought they were kind of obvious.'

'Don't ever assume that.'

'Well, I thought they all pointed to the fact that she was on her way to work, not on her way to commit suicide.'

'I agree,' he said, 'but tell me why.'

'Dressed. Made up. Had her tea. Did the dishes. Brought the paper in. Had brushed her teeth, rinsed with mouth wash, and put lipstick on.'

'You know that for sure?'

'I know about the lipstick from Jake Steinmetz. I'm guessing on the teeth brushing or mouth wash.'

'Jake could tell you that. Better find out.'

'Important?'

'Sure. Any change at all in her morning routine could blow your theory. Anything at all that even hints that her mind was elsewhere. So far, everything rings true. She was in a pattern, a habit, nothing changed. That's not how suicides work. They might get dressed up or do a few habitual things, but not everything. What would be the point? And what would it say about her state of mind?'

'Jim, I'm saying the woman was doing what she always did. She was on her way to work.'

'Why did she take a pill, Jennifer? If someone forced her, they had to have been there. And if they were there, someone would have seen them. And they would have had to have known her habits, her schedule, when she did what. Any evidence of that?'

Jennifer thought. 'No. I'll ask around, but up to now, no. Nothing like that. You know my theory on that?'

'Hm.'

'That pill was in her aspirin bottle, and it was a time bomb. Someone planted it — who knows how long ago — and waited for her to get to it.'

'Would Leo remember if she had a headache the night before? Or that morning?'

'I'll check. Why?'

'Maybe it wasn't even a bottle she always carried with her. Maybe it was a common bottle they had in the cabinet in the bathroom. If she had a headache, she might have grabbed a tablet and tossed the bottle in her bag for the work day.'

'Could be. And if so, what are you thinking?'

'You sure they didn't plant it in the bottle when the bottle was in the cabinet?'

'Jim! It sounds like you're still thinking it could have been Leo!'

'Not at all. What I'm suggesting is that the intended *victim* could have been Leo.'

8 Jennifer knew she'd hit an area of trouble the minute she walked into the Hargreaves Pharmacy on Western Avenue a few blocks from Leo's house. It was as if she was expected.

As soon as she mentioned wanting to ask some questions, she saw movement in the back, and by the time she mentioned her name, her newspaper, and the name Stanton, someone was out the door, and the ledger book was pulled off the counter.

Angry and full of adrenalin, Jennifer spotted a service entrance and dashed outside just in time to see an older man getting into a car, a raincoat over his white coat.

She ran up to the car door before he could shut it and leaned in, daring him to slam it on her. 'You must be Mr. Hargreaves,' she said sweetly.

'That's right,' he said, shoulders slumping, hands in his lap.

'Apparently you know what I want to talk to you about.'

He nodded miserably. 'Do you know this could ruin a family business that's been in this neighbourhood more'n fifty years?'

'What could?'

'What you want to talk to me about.'

'What do I want to talk to you about?'

'You tell me.'

'Let's stop playing games, Mr. Hargreaves. You've as much as admitted that your pharmacy made available drugs that killed someone. Why not just tell me about it?'

'For the paper? I don't have to talk, you know.'

'Off-the-record. For my peace of mind. And the husband's peace of mind. For your peace of mind too, I imagine.'

That struck a chord with the old man. 'Take a ride with me,' he said. She ran around and jumped in the other side.

He drove to a muddy public park where babysitters watched day care centre kids playing on the swings and bars. He turned off the engine and swung his right knee up onto the seat beside him.

Jennifer guessed him at about retirement age. He was dark complexioned and had long, wavy, salt-and-pepper hair. His accent had a faint British clip to it. He sounded weary.

'I ran errands for my father in the twenties in that shop,' he said.

She nodded.

'I'd hate to see anything happen to it. If you'll tell me again you're not going to print this in the paper, maybe I *can* tell you something that will help everybody concerned.'

She nodded again.

'Well,' he said with a sigh, 'we have rules. We're pretty strict. Have to be. State agencies are tougher on us all the time with all the drugs problems and everything. The people who work for me are either family or they're carefully trained. I mean, the family is trained too, you understand, but they're making a career of it. Everyone has to take all the courses, pass all the tests, get all the apprentice licences and all that.'

'I see.'

'What I'm getting at is this. Yes, sometimes we make an exception, do somebody a favour. But there are a lot of prerequisites, if you know what I mean.'

'Tell me.'

'For instance, I might fill a prescription two or even three times past what the doctor has indicated on the slip. But, nobody else in the shop can do it. They have to call me. And first, I have to know the customer.'

'And the doctor?'

'That goes without saying. I would never, ever fill a prescription from a doctor who didn't have references, a local address, all that, at least with your dangerous drugs.'

'OK.'

'So, I'm at home, all right? I get a call early one evening from one of my nephews. A good kid. A little young, but a lot of promise. Goes by the book. I like him. He'll make it. He asks me if he can give Mrs. Stanton a few grams of something. It was nothing, but it was a puzzle because she had phoned in first. Said she had had to get it somewhere else last time for some reason — which puzzled me because she comes to us all the time, and we're usually open.

'But anyway, she's told my nephew that she needed a little more and that she would read it to him from off the prescription slip. He'd asked her if there was a filling limit. She'd said no. Now normally, he could have filled that because she would then bring the slip in, and he would match it with the dosage and everything would be kosher.

'But the reason he calls me is that she's done all this, but when she gets there, she's forgotten the slip. She says she'll bring it in sometime, and he knows I'll have his hide if he doesn't check with me.'

'So what did you do?'

'Without a second thought, I thanked him, praised him for calling me, told him "no problem, it's always best to call." '

'And?'

'And I tell him to give her the prescription and don't make a big deal about bringing the prescription in. We don't want to treat her like we don't trust her, a longtime customer like that.'

'When did you realize you'd given her something that would prove lethal?'

'Not till I heard about her suicide. I'm tellin'

you, I cried. I was scared. I still am. I'm kickin' myself. Not that I could have stopped her. A woman wants to kill herself, she's going to do it with or without my help, you understand. But if I'd been firm, not made exceptions for an old customer and a respected doctor, who knows? Maybe I could have slowed her down, made her think twice. You know.'

'Did you check with her doctor?'

'Billings? I was afraid to. What if he says, "No, I never prescribed that" — which he probably didn't, because by itself it's virtually worthless. Then he would find out I filled a bogus prescription, and there goes my credibility with him, let alone everyone else.'

'Aren't you curious to know where she got the other ingredient?'

'Sure. I assumed it would be from the pharmacy up here on Kedzie, being so close, but again, I wasn't going to call and ask.'

'Did Mrs. Stanton pay by cheque or put it on her account?'

'Neither. She paid cash. That was a little unusual, come to think of it, because she has an active account with us. Her husband usually picks up the medicine though. But it *was* a small amount, so I didn't think anything of it.'

Jennifer was crushed, and it showed.

'I'm sorry,' he said. 'I feel terrible about it too.'

'It's not that Mr. Hargreaves. I appreciate your telling me, and I understand why you'd be scared. It's just that up to this moment, I didn't believe Mrs. Stanton committed suicide.'

He nodded slightly, understanding. 'And now you have to tell her husband?'

'Eventually.'

'I wish there was a way you could tell him that we did it in good faith, if you have to tell him.'

'I believe you did it in good faith. There's no doubt it was her, was there, sir?'

'Not really, no. It's kind of embarrassing, but I always thought Mrs. Stanton was a pretty nice looking woman. Didn't you? Did you know her?'

'Yes. Yes I did, and yes she was.'

'Well, I asked my nephew when he had her standin' right there in the shop, I says, "Is she a good-lookin' redhead?" and he kinda whispered into the phone, "That's her, Unc." '

Jennifer used an entirely different strategy at the Allen Drugs chain store adjacent to the big supermarket on Kedzie. Knowing it was a huge place that used a lot of employees, she just marched up to the counter and asked to see the head pharmacist.

'He's off until tomorrow, ma'am.'

'Then I'd like to talk to someone who has the authority to let me look through your prescription records for the last two months. I'm from the *Day*, and I'm exercising my right based on the Freedom of Information Act.'

The young man looked concerned but huddled with an associate pharmacist for a few seconds. The associate approached. 'How many I help you?' he asked.

'Exactly the way he told you,' she said firmly.

'May I see some identification?' he asked.

Jennifer pointed to the front page of the *Day*, which was in a stand near the counter. He looked at the picture of her on the front page, along with the note that she was on assignment. He smiled. 'You're prettier in person,' he said.

She didn't respond, which seemed to upset him. 'I still need to see some identification,' he said coldly. She showed him her press card and driver's licence. He studied them briefly and pushed them back to her, and as she replaced them in her wallet, he slid the big book around towards her so she could see it.

He said, 'You know that the Freedom of Information Act doesn't give you the right to print any of those actual names without permission.'

'Journalism one-oh-one,' she said, and immediately felt that had been too cold. She added a wink and a smile. He blushed and walked away.

Within seconds, Jennifer located the notation for the small amount of the ingredient needed to make a lethal dose. The date matched the one from Hargreaves, and the doctor was listed as Billings. 'An appropriate name for a doctor,' Leo had once joked, but now it didn't seem so funny.

Next to the listing, however, was a notation. *No prescription. Verified with phys. by phone. Pd. cash.*

Dr. Floyd Billings was a stocky, pleasant, soft-spoken man who agreed to meet Jennifer at the end of his office hours, about six-thirty. He loosened his coat and sat across the desk from her in a small examining room.

'I was as shocked as anyone when Mrs. Stanton took her own life,' he said. 'I knew she had not told her husband of her problem, but I assume she left him a note.'

'There was no note, doctor. That's why we've been convinced it was not a suicide. What was her problem?'

'Oh, I'm afraid I would not be at liberty to say, even though she's dead. That is very privileged information. She made me pledge not to tell her husband, a pledge I would now break. But you understand that I couldn't tell you.'

'But you would tell Leo?'

'I would.'

'I understand. Could you at least tell me if her problem was terminal?'

'I really shouldn't discuss it. I'm sorry.'

'Dr. Billings, do you recall receiving a phone call — it would have been two months ago to the day yesterday — from Allen Drugs?'

'Well, I get so many — '

'Mrs. Stanton was there without a prescription, but they called you to verify that it was all right to give her the medicine.'

He furrowed his brow. 'I *do* recall something like that. Yes! I remember.'

'Do you recall what the medicine was?'

'I didn't ask.'

'Excuse me?'

'I didn't ask. I had my girl look up her charts

quickly and tell me if we had prescribed any-thing out of the ordinary lately. She said no, so I told the druggist to refill whatever she was asking for.'

'Would you like to see what she asked for?'

He nodded and leaned forward to take the small slip of paper from Jennifer. Reading it, he winced and paled. He carefully laid the paper on the desk in front of him and ran his fingers over his face.

'She was a patient of mine for decades,' he said, his voice weak. 'I mean it. At least three decades. She must have had a breakdown of some sort. She must have.'

'You've said you were shocked when you heard of her death, and you can't believe she would do something like this after you had known her for so long, so I'm guessing that what-ever physical problem she, might have had was not terminal. Otherwise this might have all made some sense to you. Am I right?'

'I'd rather not discuss it. Are you going to report me for this lack of discretion? In retro-spect, of course, I can see what a terrible mistake I made. Those precautions we're supposed to use are to protect us from drug addicts, not our own patients.'

'I don't think anything would be served by my telling anyone. When you tell Mr. Stanton about his wife's problem, you might want to tell him these details.'

'Perhaps you're right. I don't look forward to that.'

'You'll have some time,' she said.

Jennifer didn't look forward to talking to Leo again herself.

9 The next morning, Jennifer phoned Leo's Wisconsin cottage. As expected, Mark answered.

'Is Leo furious?' Jennifer asked.

'Well, I don't think he cares to speak to you, if that's what you mean.'

'Are you serious?'

Mark didn't respond, and Jennifer was worried.

'Mark, I need to know if your mother was ill, either in the night before she died or that morning. Was there a headache or any other sort of ailment? Can you find out from your father and let me know? I want to know why she took an aspirin.'

Mark was silent.

'Mark?' she said tentatively.

'Hm.'

'Are you there?'

'I miss you,' he said, flatly.

She pursed her lips. She was thinking, *Oh, for pete's sake, grow up. You're acting like a child! I'm engaged, I'm busy, and I don't have time for fun and games right now.* But she didn't respond. She decided she could play the game the same way he did. She decided there was nothing quite as frustrating as being ignored by phone.

She pretended Mark hadn't said anything. 'Can you find out for me?' she repeated.

'I know how you feel about me,' he said, desperately.

That's a laugh, she thought, pitying him.

'And you'll either call me or have your father call me, OK?'

'Bye-bye,' Mark said endearingly.

Jennifer nearly threw up. This was all she needed in the middle of a frustrating and disappointing investigation. She was trying to muster the courage she would need to tell Leo the bad news — that his wife had indeed apparently stretched the truth to the breaking point to get the combination of contraband drugs that killed her.

Jennifer spent the rest of the morning studying her notes, wondering where to turn and what to look for that might make the evidence look less certain. She and Jim would be going to a prayer meeting at their church that night. She had already requested prayer for her boss, whose wife had died. But how could she ask for prayer that it was other than a suicide?

She finally decided to console herself by making an appointment to talk to someone who would probably agree with her — someone who would feel too that, in spite of all the evidence, Samantha Stanton could not have taken her own life. She called Mrs. Stanton's best friend.

June Roloff invited her to lunch. 'As long as you don't put yourself out,' Jennifer said.

'Nonsense,' she said in a pleasantly low voice.

'I could just as easily pick you up and take you out somewhere,' Jennifer suggested.

'Really, it'll be no problem,' Mrs. Roloff said.

Jennifer had met the striking fifty-year-old brunette before, but she had not realized what a smart neighbourhood the Roloffs lived in, or even that they had domestic help. Their exquisite lunch of light crepes and fresh fruit was served as they sat on a wrought iron and glass balcony.

Jennifer wanted to blurt out the question: Where in their world did the Roloffs get the money for a place like that? But she just tried to take it in her stride. It was apparent that Mrs. Roloff was still grieving. Her eyes filled with tears whenever she reminisced about Samantha.

'I'm being asked to teach her class and even to lead some of her travel tours now,' she said. 'I just don't know if I can, or if I should.'

'Why not?' Jennifer asked. 'It would be for her, wouldn't it?'

'I suppose, maybe. Yes, it might. But it would be so painful, so difficult. I'm not another Samantha, and I don't want to pretend to be.'

The woman spent much of the afternoon talking about her many adventures with Samantha. 'We travelled quite a bit together, you know.'

Jennifer nodded.

'She left a little piece of Gateway to me,' June said. 'I was so touched, I cried and cried. It was so sweet of her.'

'When did you find out?' Jennifer asked. 'I was under the impression that the will had not been executed yet.'

'Oh, it hasn't, but Samantha told me she was going to do that about six months ago. She even showed me a copy of the will.'

'You must have been very moved.'

'It was unlike any feeling in the world. That agency had become her life, outside of Leo, of course. She couldn't have left me anything more personal unless she had left me her family.'

And she clouded over again.

'Mrs. Roloff, I know you're upset, but I want to confide in you, and I have to admit, the news is not good. May I?'

'I guess so.'

'I've been researching this death under the assumption that Samantha Stanton would be the last person in the world to commit suicide. I admit I was biased. I was looking for the evidence I wanted to find. Much of it is puzzling, but the majority is troubling.'

'In what way?'

'In that it is becoming apparent that Mrs. Stanton may have indeed taken her own life.'

'And that surprises you?' Mrs. Roloff asked.

'Your response surprises me,' Jennifer said.

'Why?'

'Well, I, because I just assumed, I mean — I didn't think you thought it was suicide.'

'Why not?'

'Because you knew her. Leo lived with her, and he's convinced it wasn't suicide.'

'If it wasn't suicide, what was it?' Mrs. Roloff said. 'An accident?'

'I was thinking more in terms — '

'Because if it wasn't an accident or suicide, it was murder, and one thing I'm certain of, Sam didn't have any enemies — at least not any who would have murdered her.'

'Who were her enemies?'

'I wouldn't even know that. I know she had some run-ins with certain stockholders in her company, but nothing serious. She always speculated that one of the representatives of one of the owners was in league with some old couple on the board, but I never got any of the specifics, and it certainly didn't sound like she had developed any serious conflicts.'

'Then you think it was an accident, Mrs. Roloff?'

June Roloff stood and stared out from the balcony at her withering garden. 'You mistake grief and loss for naiveté,' she said. 'You forget that we were like sisters.'

Jennifer was shocked. 'Are you telling me you think she committed suicide?'

'I try not to think about it,' she said.

'But were you close enough to know what Dr. Billings knew?'

'Of course. I always thought she should have told Leo. It wasn't going to kill her. The sugar in her blood would eventually affect her eyesight. It already had, of course. But she was a lot of years from hardening of the arteries. She had a lot of good years left. Maybe as many as twenty.'

'Why do you think she didn't tell Leo?'

'I think she thought it would make her less of a woman. She was within a year of having to give herself insulin injections. I don't think she was quite ready for that.'

'I still don't see her killing herself.'

'It's hard for me too,' Mrs. Roloff said. 'Though not totally surprising.'

'Why haven't you told Leo?'

'I didn't know if he really didn't believe it, or if he simply wasn't accepting it. He will eventually. He needs his illusions right now.'

'Then I'm wild-goose chasing.'

'Jennifer, there is nothing that would please me more than for you to discover that I'm wrong. It horrifies me to think that she's gone, and to add the nightmare that she is gone by her own hand when Leo and I and so many loved her so deeply. I just don't want to accept that either. But it happened, and I'm trying to cope. Keep searching until you're satisfied.'

'But you're implying that I am not going to like what I find.'

'You haven't so far.'

'For the most part, no.'

'For the most part?'

'Well, there was shoddy police work that could have messed things up. There was the fact that Samantha wasn't despondent, that Leo or anyone knew of anyway.' Jennifer's listener betrayed a sad, knowing smile. 'And she was all ready for work when she died. Why?'

'Probably because she didn't want anyone to notice,' June said. 'She wasn't the type to do anything for show. She wouldn't have faked an attempt just to get Leo's attention. She did it so it would be discovered after it was done. That's my guess.'

'That must be very difficult for you to even think about.'

'Right.'

'Is there more?' Jennifer asked.

'More?'

'More reason to believe it was suicide and not an accident or murder.'

'Well, a person doesn't accidentally kill herself with a dose like that one. That rules out accidents, unless it was intended for Leo, and everyone knows that's ludicrous.'

Jennifer nodded. 'But couldn't it still have been murder?'

'That's almost as painful to consider as suicide.'

'But we have to consider it, Mrs. Roloff. Because if it was murder and everyone thinks it's suicide, that means there's a murderer around somewhere. Someone who knew an awful lot about Samantha Stanton's habits.'

'Don't go implicating Leo now,' Mrs. Roloff said.

'I wouldn't think of it,' Jennifer said. 'Never.'

They sat in silence for several minutes.

'Anything else that will help me?' Jennifer asked finally.

'Nothing you'll be happy about,' she said.

'I'll be happy for anything that will bring an end to this assignment I once so eagerly wanted.'

'Even if it ends the way you don't want it to?'

'I'm afraid so now. I just have to know, one way or the other.'

'You'll need to keep this confidential.'

'Of course.'

'From everyone.'

'Everyone?'

'Absolutely.'

'Let me think about that for a moment.' Jennifer had the feeling that Samantha's best friend in the world could shed some light on the truth, that she might say something that would be difficult to take, but that there was something to the cliché that the truth hurts. 'All right,' she said, 'I'll keep your confidence.'

'How do you think Samantha got those euthanasia booklets?'

Jennifer blinked. 'I've been hoping to prove that they were planted by a murderer.'

'In a way, I wish you were right. Like I said, knowing she was murdered is not any more pleasant than knowing she killed herself, but somehow I feel so guilty about her suicide.'

Jennifer wanted to hear where June Roloff

thought Samantha had got the suicide manuals, but she couldn't let that comment go. '*You* feel guilty about it?'

'Certainly. I was her best friend. Her confidante. I was committed to her. I had responsibilities and obligations to her.' She began to cry. 'And she did to me too!'

'Such as?'

'She had a commitment, a responsibility to stay alive. I resent that she's gone! I need her! I loved her and cared about her and gave of myself for her. And she did to me too, until this. Leaving without so much as a note or a good-bye — I can hardly bear it.'

'But she left you that most personal gift.'

'That was a gesture that came long before she died. It was sweet and thoughtful, but I didn't want it this way.'

'But why should you feel guilty?'

'Because I was inadequate. I wasn't what she needed. I wasn't enough! She had such deep needs and causes, and I was not up to the challenge. Because she couldn't find answers anywhere — not even in me — she left us all.'

Mrs. Roloff hid her eyes with her hand, but Jennifer had to ask. 'Do you know where she got the booklets?'

The older woman nodded, her tear-streaked face finally showing its age. 'She dragged me out to one secret meeting of the SMS. You know, Sam and I agreed a lot philosophically, but we parted there.'

'The SMS?'

'Simplified Method Society.'

'Method of what?'

'Self-euthanasia. Assisted-euthanasia. Call it whatever you like. They advocate suicide as a humane method of death for the terminally ill, or really for anyone who chose it and didn't want it to be painful or messy.'

'You actually went with her?'

'She badgered me for ages to go. Asked me to think about it. To consider it. She hit me with dozens of hypothetical situations. What if this and what if that? Some of them were hard to argue with. I suppose there would be situations where I would rather be put out of my misery, even by a friend or relative than to suffer on for years.'

'Where does a group like that meet?'

'In local hotels or restaurants. When you come in, they ask if you know what they meet to talk about and to promote. If you say no, they tell you you're not welcome. If you say yes, they ask you to state it briefly. If you're right, you may come in.'

'What's the purpose of all that?'

'To make sure no one gets in the wrong room, is then shocked and tells someone who won't understand what it's all about.'

'And they distribute this literature?'

'Free. But not to me. No, ma'am. I even used a phony name when I attended. I got the impression most people did. Not Sam though. Nobody could make Sam pretend she was someone else. So there was ol' Samantha Stanton, visiting the

euthanasia meeting with her frumpy friend
Claudia Brown.'

'Frumpy?'

'I even disguised myself, Jennifer! New name
and new look. It was creepy, and I never went
back.' She began to become emotional again.
'You see why I can't be terribly surprised at her
death — at least her method?'

10

'I agree it looks bleak,' Jim said after the prayer meeting that night as he and Jennifer strolled along a Lake Michigan beach. Strolled might not be the word for it. She huddled against him and hid her face and neck from the chilling wind — happy to be with him, but regretting the choice of the beach.

Finally they sought shelter behind a gigantic tree trunk about sixty feet from the water's edge and settled in the sand with their backs against the wood. Out of the wind and nestled against Jim's chest, Jennifer felt relaxed and secure in the silence.

She had told him the story of her day while they rode to and from the church. 'These people seem so empty,' she said. 'Leo and his son and even Samantha. Mrs. Fritzee. Mrs. Roloff. It's depressing.'

'Seems it would give you a chance to talk to them about God,' he said.

'You'd think so, and I know this sounds like an excuse, but I start listening to them and empathizing with them, and I get emotional and can't bring myself to tell them of the most important things. I'm overwhelmed with how they're looking in the wrong place for their peace and their answers, but so much so that it's as if I'm incapacitated.'

He nodded in sympathy. 'What are you thinking now about Samantha's death?'

She shook her head. 'I don't know any more. I just don't know.'

'That's a good sign,' he said. 'Good or bad, depending upon how you look at it.'

'What do you mean?'

'I mean it's apparent you haven't made up your mind yet, even though you have evidence heavily weighted one way. That's healthy scepticism in my book; it might be delusion to some people. That's why it's good or bad, depending — '

'My guess is I'm deluding myself, Jim.' He didn't respond. It was *her* theory, not his. She continued. 'The only reason I think it could still be murder is that her morning routine didn't change one iota and because I knew the woman.'

'You *thought* you knew the woman,' he said.

She nodded. 'Leo thought he knew the woman too.'

'I would agree with Leo.'

'But Jim, Leo says she didn't commit suicide.'

'I'd say he knows better than anyone.'

'You agree with him?'

'That's what I said.'

'I do too.'

'I know you do, Jenn.'

'How did you know?'

'Besides the fact that it's written all over you?'

'Uh-huh.'

'Because you're staring at two pharmacies, a doctor, a best friend, a coroner, the cops, and the evidence, and they all say it was suicide. Yet you're undecided. To me, that's not undecided. To me, you're coming down on the side of murder.'

'But why am I, Jim? Am I that clever — or that stupid?'

'I'd like to think your intuition is good. It could be blind loyalty to your boss.'

'Which he could also be guilty of Jim: blind loyalty to his wife.'

'Right. But I am sure of this, the truth will surface. It always does.'

'Always?'

'As long as people keep looking for it.'

'How long will I have to look?'

'That's entirely up to you.'

'And up to my bosses,' she said. Jim chuckled.

'I'm not sure I know where to turn next.'

'That's a detective's greatest position,' he said. 'When you don't know where to turn next, turn everywhere. Get general. Stop being so specific.

Think of all the places and people you've heard about so far, what you've learned, what questions have been raised. Anything you're thinking or wondering about?'

'Yeah,' she said. 'I'd like to meet some of the people behind Gateway Travel. I'd like to check again with the coroner to find out about toothpaste or mouth wash in Mrs. Stanton's body. I want to hear back from Casanova about whether his father remembers if his mother had a headache sometime just before her death.'

'Go for all of 'em, Jenn, but don't leave out an important one.'

'I'm listening.'

'Hadn't you better attend an SMS meeting?'

'In disguise, of course.'

'Of course.'

Coroner Jacob Steinmetz, M.D., stared at Jennifer from over the tops of his half-glasses the next morning in his office. 'I said nothing about sugar content in the blood,' he said, 'and I dare say her personal doctor didn't either.'

Jennifer just returned his gaze.

'We noted something about the eye muscle and tissue,' he said. 'That's all, if your sugar guess is based on the transcript of the autopsy. You can't necessarily assume diabetes based on glaucoma.'

'Any evidence she was a marijuana user?'

'That would be extremely difficult to determine by autopsy unless she had inhaled the smoke shortly before death. We didn't find any such trace. Why?'

'Isn't it common for glaucoma sufferers to even be *prescribed* marijuana?'

'Not common. Bandied about in sensational journals, I suppose. But no, not common in this country. Don't impugn a fine doctor like Billings. He's a good man.'

'Tell me about the residue on her teeth or gums.'

'Standard. Food particles. Tooth paste. Mouth wash.'

'Alcohol?'

'Only from the mouth wash.'

'How do you know that?'

'From the amount. C'mon, Jennifer, you're fishing. Let's get on with this so I can get back to work, huh? I wish *you* would too. I like you better when you're interviewing me for a story, not as an amateur detective.'

'That hurt,' she said, seriously. He didn't respond. She quickly recovered and plunged ahead. 'I want to know,' she said, 'if you could tell whether Mrs. Stanton had a headáche within twelve hours of her death or whether the poison would have obliterated such evidence.'

'No, the poison would not have duplicated the blood vessel trauma created by a headache. However, death sometimes releases the pressure on the brain, and the headache symptoms go away.'

'Was that the case in her death?'

'Why are you curious about a headache, Jennifer?'

'Well, I don't know, but apparently my hunch was right, because you're already evading the question.'

'I won't evade it if you'll tell me where you're going with this.'

'You've got a deal. You first.'

'The woman was suffering from a severe headache, just short of a migraine, possibly up to six hours before her death. There's evidence she took some aspirin in the middle of the night.'

'I don't recall that from our first conversation, Jake.'

'We didn't have a deal then, Jennifer.'

'Must I always make a deal to get straight answers?'

'Always,' he said, smiling. 'Now what're you making of all this?'

'The woman was murdered, Jake. Someone slipped a bogus pill into her aspirin bottle. If she wanted to kill herself, why not in the middle of the night while her head was throbbing?'

'Maybe she didn't want her husband to wake up next to her corpse.'

'And maybe I'm right,' she said.

'So you're saying someone slipped the pill into her bottle, possibly a long time before her death. Because they couldn't know when she was going to have a headache.'

'I guess so.'

'Unless they poisoned her just a little the day before to make her feel the need of an aspirin.' He was teasing her, and she resented it. 'And how were they to know that she wouldn't share the bottle with her husband and wind up killing him unintentionally? Really, Jennifer, you're barking up the wrong — '

'The woman was dressed for work, Jake, and she completed her morning routine right through to the tooth brushing and the mouth wash.'

'And if the murderer planted the suicide pill, how did he know when to plant the euthanasia booklets so it would look like a suicide?'

Jennifer didn't know what to say. A murderer would have had no way of knowing when Mrs. Stanton would take the fatal pill, so how *could* the books have been planted?

Jennifer stood. 'I'm going to prove Samantha Stanton didn't kill herself, Jake. But it won't be out of any malice towards you. Can we still be friends, no matter how it turns out?'

He smiled weakly. 'Sure. Just promise me you won't have the body exhumed. I hate disinterred bodies. Messy all the way around. Families don't like it. Nobody does.'

'I promise to avoid that if possible,' she said, knowing Leo would probably oppose it too. That is, unless he felt it was absolutely necessary to clear his wife's name.

Mr. T.J. Rand — even by telephone from Texas — was not at all what Jennifer expected. She thought he'd be a big-talking loudmouth with a twangy drawl. The drawl was there all right, but with no twang, no volume, and no bragging.

'I don't rightly know why Mr. Dennison is makin' a bid now for Mr. Griffin's share. But I cain't hardly blame the man for sellin', now that the principal owner has died and we'll be lookin' frantically for a new working manager, understand?'

'Will you be selling too?'

'Oh my, no!' came the shrill voice of Kimberly Rand, whom Jennifer had not known was even on the line. 'Things may never be better! We're still happy with our investment, and frankly, I can get excited about Mr. Dennison's clients taking a little more control in the company.'

Jennifer decided to go on the offensive. 'There are those who suspect that Mr. Dennison actually represents some other stockholder and that the purchase will then represent an even larger portion of the company.'

'I have to get off now, T.J.,' Kimberly said. 'I got no more time for speculation with someone I don't even know. You get off the phone soon too, you hear?'

'Yes, dear. Well, Miz Grey, I never really thought o' that. But if the company that Mr. Dennison represents is actually a front for one of the other smaller stockholders, it could only be us. If it was Griffin, he'd be buyin' himself out. Dennison's K.R.C. Limited owns two small shares, so that leaves only us to be the sneaky partner. Is that what you're implyin'?'

'Yes, sir.'

'Well, I resent that. First of all, you shoulda just come out an' said it. Second of all, I don't know how you get K.R.C. out of T.J. Rand. Good day, Miz Grey.'

Jennifer's appointment with the seller, Wilfred Griffin, was for the mid-afternoon. She found him in his suburban Niles office, which also housed several similar firms. Griffin was one member of a five-principal company that invested mainly in municipal bonds.

'But this deal,' he said brightly, with a big smile she assumed was normal, 'is strictly independent, strictly personal. I'm rather proud of it. On my own, even when I was a junior member of this firm and didn't have my name on the stationery, I tried to get them to invest in Gateway Travel. It was voted down twice out of hand, and then I was allowed to pitch for it officially, I mean with the whole dog and pony show, you know what I mean?' He didn't wait for a response.

'I mean I had Mrs. Stanton in here, and I had flip charts and slides and earning curves and flowcharts and graphs. I'm tellin' ya, if I'd been an investor, I'd have jumped at it.'

'But they didn't?'

'No, they didn't. But did I rub it in when I invested on my own and made a nice piece of change? No, ma'am. Not my style. I didn't even brag about it. But I *did* make it clear I had taken a chance on my own, just so I could kinda live and die by that one risk — 'course, I was convinced it was safe and in fact had great potential — '

'I gathered that.'

'Huh? Ha! Yeah! I guess you would. Any-hoo, I never bragged about quarterly or annual earnings unless someone asked. But when they asked, as they always did — independent of each other and always claiming that if it had been solely up to them, they would have voted for it — I was ready with a little printout to show just how successful and profitable it had been for me. They're all a bunch of liars, of course, because the vote was unanimous against it every time. I mean *every* time. But I don't mind. Those are the kind of lies I tell too. None of us are actually dishonest; in fact, our firm is honest to a fault. Never cheated a client. Never will. But fudge a little on your own reputation, well — you know what I mean. That's why I was always ready with the printout, because no one would have believed me otherwise.

'Why, would you believe that each and every one of them at one time or another has asked how they can buy into the company *and* whether they can buy *me* out! Would you believe that?'

'Every *one* of them?'

'Every one.'

'No, I wouldn't believe that.'

'Well, you catch on fast, sweetie, 'cause you're right. Only three of the four have asked to buy me out, but they've all asked the other questions. Believe me?'

'Never again,' she said laughing. 'I'll never trust another investment banker as long as I live.'

He laughed too. 'Now, what can I do for you? You're probably wonderin' why in the world this idiot is selling out. I'll tell you straight. I got an offer I couldn't refuse. I got an offer twice what the stock is worth. It's such a good offer that I'm not even worried — and I know the buyer isn't worried in the least — that the other owners will even come close to it. 'Course they won't know what it is, so they'll be at a disadvantage. But I'll bet no one comes within fifty per cent of it when they try to *beat* it.'

'So, strictly a money deal.'

'Exactly.'

11 Jennifer's hope that there was something to chew on in the relationship between Wilfred ('Call me Freddie') Griffin and Samantha Stanton was short-lived.

'I just admired the woman, that's all. Met her husband once. Whale of a nice guy, and talented newspaperman, I understand. But this woman ran that agency like a pro from the day she bought in and became the manager. She'd been there before, you know, but after she came up through the ranks to assistant manager, she had to scrape up some money somewhere and buy in to become manager.'

'Was there a problem with the previous manager?' Jennifer asked.

'None, except that the board disliked him. I wasn't there then; this is all hearsay. 'Course,

K.R.C. never liked anything or anybody in management, so when I came I tried to balance 'em out a little. Never worked.

'They were right in that case, though, and when Mrs. Stanton bought in and took over, profits went up right away. Wasn't long, though, before Conrad Dennison became the representative for the holding company, and he was more demanding than the last guy.'

'Do you happen to know where Mrs. Stanton got her money?'

Griffin smiled. 'Sure. She told us plenty of times. It was one-third inheritance, one-third saved up, and one-third borrowed, long since paid off. Remarkable woman.'

'Truly. Do you think there was trouble between Mrs. Stanton and the previous manager?'

'Nah. Just the usual frustrations of workin' for somebody who doesn't do as good a job as you could do. We all deal with that, don't we? Ha!'

'But there's no lingering problem that you know of?'

'Oh, no. I don't even remember the guy's name, but he became a ticket counter man at one of the big airlines at O'Hare. Died about three years ago. Heart attack, I think. I got his name in the file if you want it.'

Jennifer shook her head. 'Do you think Mrs. Stanton had any enemies on the board?'

Griffin's smile faded and he squinted at her. 'You mean *real* enemies? Like murderin' enemies? No. None. We had our squabbles, but

no, not at all. Not even Dennison, and he was her
biggest critic.'

'We'll see,' Jennifer said. 'Now, Mr. Griffin,
I've looked over several sets of minutes of your
meetings over the past few years, and I have to
ask you why you finally relented and will sell to
Dennison. I know the money was good, but aren't
you worried about the character of the
company?'

'Not really. I know what you're thinking, and I
know I've been less than cordial in disagreeing
with Mr. Dennison a lot in the meetings, but my
share won't give K.R.C. Limited enough power to
do anything. Unless he thinks he can buy out the
Stanton heir, he's not really helped himself
except financially. And despite how much he
paid me, if they can find the right manager, he'll
have his money inside a decade.'

'A decade? Isn't that a long wait?'

'Not for that kind of dough. 'Course, K.R.C.
couldn't have known that Mrs. Stanton was
going to die, but I'm not going to let him out of
the offer. He may try to pull some legal she-
nanigan now, but I've got him by the short hairs. I
was going to turn him down, you know, even at
the price he settled at.'

'You were?'

''Course I was!'

'What changed your mind?'

'What else? Mrs. Stanton's death.'

'You wouldn't have sold even for a big price
with her running the show?'

'Nope. Said that many times. I think Mr.

Dennison has bought himself a pig in a poke now, but that's his problem.'

'Do you think Mrs. Stanton committed suicide?'

'Well, yeah! 'Course! I didn't know that was even a question. I didn't really know the woman enough to know what was troubling her. She certainly couldn't have had money problems unless she was way overextended. But we'd have known if the agency wasn't in tip-top shape, and it always was. I don't know why she killed herself.'

'You can't consider the possibility that it was not a suicide?'

'Hm, I don't know. I guess not after seein' the news and readin' the paper. Nah. It was a suicide all right. You got any evidence says it wasn't?'

'Not enough,' she said.

He smiled at her. 'Pity. I liked her. Didn't know her well, but admired her. Seemed a good woman, and she sure was a good agency manager. I owe her a lot. In fact, I owe her double, triple maybe. Gettin' out when she got out is gonna make me richer than the agency ever did in the past, and that wasn't half bad. Gotta admit I had perfect timing this time.'

'Getting out when she got out?'

'I didn't mean any disrespect by that. Just a manner of speaking. I really was shocked and sad when I heard she was gone, and gone that way. Depressed me for a while. But I was sure glad I hadn't turned down K.R.C.'s offer. I was about to, but when I heard the news, I sat on it.'

Jennifer felt a little sleazy leaving Griffin's office. He had, at first, seemed so bright and optimistic. He fit the image she had built of him from reading the minutes of the meetings.

But in the end he was the same as most of the other financial wizards she knew: out for himself, caring only about the bottom line, the buck. It was disappointing.

She had an evening appointment with Conrad Dennison in his North Sheridan Road office, but a message on her phone answering machine made her call to change that to the next morning.

'Jennifer, this is Jim,' the recording said, 'and there's an SMS meeting tonight. Check your newspaper's personal column.'

With Leo coming back around noon the next day, she wanted to have all her facts straight. It would be bad enough facing him with bad news (and after having opened his mail), but she certainly wanted to have enough information so that she knew for sure whether Samantha Stanton had taken her own life or was murdered.

She didn't need a suspect — just a clue.

Tossing her raincoat over the edge of the sofa, she grabbed a piece of chicken from the refrigerator and laid out the newspaper on the table with her other hand.

Jim was right. In among all the love notes and prayers for the now departed, she found a simple message. 'SMS tonight. Surf and Turf Inn. Estes Avenue. 7 p.m. Word to the wise.'

She didn't want to go alone. She didn't want to be recognized. Of course, she would not use her real name. But Jim couldn't go with her; he was on duty.

Jennifer rummaged around in her wardrobe and drawers for — what was it June Roloff had said? — something frumpy. The clothes and jewellery were easy. Jennifer looked frumpy all right. A bandana in her hair set the tone. But what finished the look was when she found the pink spectacle frames she had worn in high school, just before she had switched to contact lenses.

She wore her contacts to drive to Estes Avenue off Sheridan, then removed them and put on her old glasses before leaving her car some distance from the Surf and Turf. A quick glance in the mirror made her chuckle at the dowdy, middle-aged matron who peeked back.

As Jennifer walked down the rain-swept street, she caught glimpses of herself in the reflections of puddles, but her humour couldn't override her fear.

What if someone recognized her?

What if they asked for identification?

What if she saw someone she knew?

What if they didn't let her out?

What if she forgot what to say when they asked her if she knew what the meeting was about?

But she didn't. 'Euthanasia,' she said.

'Ten dollars,' the woman responded.

'Oh, my,' Jennifer said. 'I didn't expect that.'

'It gets you on our mailing list, dear. And we have expenses. Sign the book at the front on the right when you get in the room.'

No one seemed to notice when she entered, though forty or so people sat in stacking chairs in a dark-panelled room. She went and stood in line, about sixth, to sign the book. She prayed no one would stand behind her so she'd have time to peek back in the register to see if she could find Samantha's name — or June Roloff's 'Claudia Brown'.

But someone came in when Jennifer was second in line. 'Go ahead,' she said. 'I just want to tie my shoe.' He passed, and she bent down to tie the old brogue she hadn't worn for years. When she stood, no one was behind her, so she leafed through a few pages before signing, 'Louise Purcell'.

She didn't see any names she recognized, but she did see a lot of names she assumed were phonies. She had to hand *that*, at least, to Mrs. Stanton. There was no hiding for her. That's why the escape of suicide seemed so incongruous.

From the looks of the garb and the demeanour, she was guessing she was with a fairly sophisticated intellectual crowd. A spokesman began by passing the notebook around and reminding everybody to add their address so they could be on the mailing list.

As soon as she heard that, Jennifer headed for the back row where she would have time to scan the book without suspicion.

While she waited for the book to make its rounds, a black-bearded man, who appeared to be in his late thirties and who wore an Indian chain and necklace, made an announcement:

'For those of you who have been worried about our being found out and hassled and turned away from meeting rooms and such, you'll be happy to know that our lawyers, of whom there are four here tonight — raise your hands; oh, five! — are making real progress with the American Civil Liberties Union in allowing us to meet in the open and say and do what we want.'

There was a certain amount of clapping and subdued cheering. The rest of the surprisingly short meeting consisted of various updates on the chapters in other cities, recent developments in court cases, the sharing of anecdotes about terminally ill patients who suffered unmercifully for years, and more stories of people who were aided in their efforts to die peacefully.

More cheering greeted every such story, and then a list was read of people who belonged to the SMS worldwide who had died peacefully, either self-induced or aided, in the last month. There were oohs and aahs when the reader announced that there was a possibility that someone who had attended one of 'this very chapter's meetings may have died of her own choosing very recently. It was definitely done to specification and of her own volition.'

By then Jennifer was casually looking through the book and unaware of anyone noticing. Sure enough, from the beginning of the book, Samantha Stanton's name appeared on nearly every list. The night they met in Alsip, a Claudia Brown had signed, but there was no Samantha Stanton.

Jennifer couldn't work that out and assumed she had missed Samantha's name. She was searching the list one more time when someone nudged her and asked for the book.

On the way home, she detoured farther north on Sheridan Road to check out the address she'd been given for K.R.C. Limited. Her suspicion had been correct. The initials K.R.C. did not appear on the directory in the lobby. The building housed law firms.

Discovering who was represented by Conrad Dennison would be tougher than she thought. She searched the board for his name. It was there alone in suite 4404.

She scanned the board for other names in that same suite. There were three or four listed singly, as Dennison was, and there was another listing of the name of the firm itself, 'Cocharan, Thomas, Rand, and Kahill'.

Rand, she thought. *Coincidental? Has to be.* The next morning she asked.

Conrad Dennison got a big belly laugh out of that question. He had come out to the waiting room himself to invite her into his beautifully appointed office, pretty nice for someone who wasn't yet a partner.

'*Yet* is right,' he said, sitting at his desk in green suit slacks, white shirt, striped tie, and waistcoat. He also wore alligator cowboy boots. He was in his early forties and had wavy, longish hair that gave him a slightly outdated look. 'If you think *this* office is nice, you should see the partners' offices.'

He made a clicking sound with his mouth to indicate, she supposed, that they were top dog. 'But I'll be there soon enough,' he said. 'Just a matter of time. They take care of me, and I've been doing the job for them for years.'

She nodded.

'So you thought Rand was ol' T.J. Rand, did you?' he said, laughing again. 'Nope, not even close, and am I glad of that! This Rand is one of the Boston Rands,' he added, raising his eyebrows as if certain Jennifer would immediately recognize that name. She didn't.

'Tell me about K.R.C.,' she said.

He stared evenly at her, not moving. He smiled. 'What do you want to know? I thought this had to do with the travel agency.'

'Doesn't K.R.C. have anything to do with the travel agency?'

'Well, just in the sense that they own a quarter of it, that's all. I handle that for them.'

'Who are they?'

'A holding company. They have several interests.'

'Who are they?'

'Business people. A small concern with a lot of irons in a lot of fires. They do well for themselves.'

'Who are they?'

'They're private, anonymous people who, if they wanted nosy reporters to know who they were, would have used their names in their logo. Since they didn't, and since I am paid handsomely to represent them in the strictest confidence, you can stop hoping I'll suddenly spew forth the name just because you keep asking.'

She stared him down. 'Just one name?' she said.

'Name, names — what's the difference?'

'The difference is whether it's one person or more than one person. It'll make it easier for me to get the name from public records if I know a little more about this out-of-state group.'

'You're really being childish for a big city reporter, you know that? You think that by saying they're out-of-state, you're going to get me to think that you really believe that so I'll confirm that they're local. It could be one name and more than one person, you know. Or vice versa.'

'Not vice versa,' she said sweetly. 'That would be stupid. One person and several people's names? Silly.'

'Perhaps,' he said, reddening. 'Do yourself a favour and give up on the name, OK?'

'What do you suppose the odds are that Wilfred Griffin will accept your generous offer?'

Dennison flushed again and clenched his fists. 'How do you know about that?'

'I'm a big city reporter,' she said.

He softened and smiled, but his fists were still clenched. 'I'm not at liberty to speak to that either,' he said.

'Uncanny sense of timing on that offer,' she pressed. 'Would you have made it if you'd known?'

'Known what?'

'About Mrs. Stanton.'

'I didn't make the offer. I represented it.'

'Will you withdraw it now that she's out of the picture?'

'That's none of your business.'

12 Jennifer was desperate, but Dennison didn't know it. And that was all she had to go on. 'I've made it my business,' she said. 'I have to know who's behind K.R.C., and if you don't tell me, I'll find out somewhere else.'

'What's the big deal?'

'The big deal is that Mrs. Stanton, the majority owner, was murdered, and now here you are making a big play for more of the company for who knows who?'

'Whoa! First, she wasn't murdered! Second, I've always made pitches for more of the company, which a look at any of our records will prove. And third, you'll note that this latest pitch was tendered *before* she committed suicide. You think it drove her to suicide?'

'Not a chance,' Jennifer said. 'She was never

intimidated by you or the company you represented. And while she was alive, there was no way you could have dreamt of getting more than half the company. Even if you bought out both the other minority partners — which would be foolish because K.R.C. is undoubtedly in collusion with one of them — you would still have only fifty per cent.'

He sat smiling smugly at her. 'Well, if I'm in collusion with another partner, it'd have to be the Rands, wouldn't it?'

She nodded.

'I like the old girl — not so much her ol' man — but she's fun, and we think alike. Unfortunately, she's too shrewd to sell. Maybe if the business flags a little during the transition of managers, the Rands will reconsider.'

'There's nothing to the initials relating to the woman's name, is there?' Jennifer tried, feeling foolish.

But Dennison was visibly shaken. 'What are you saying?' he managed, eyes narrowing.

'I'm saying I think it's an interesting coincidence that the woman you so enjoy has the initials K.R. Could K.R.C. be the Kimberly Rand Company?'

'You're joking.'

'You're stalling.'

'No! Of course not! How could she have me representing her business without her husband's knowledge? Well, let me just say you're not going to get any information out of me, but I'll give you my solemn promise and guarantee, K.R.C. Limited has no more to do with the Rands, either of them, than it does with our own firm.'

'And why should I believe you?'

'Maybe you shouldn't. You decide. You're not going to find out one way or the other anyway. But let me save you some time and trouble in your little mission; forget the Rands. I'm serious.'

'You only make me want to focus right on them,' she said.

He shrugged and raised his hands in surrender. 'Suit yourself,' he said.

On her way out she paused at the directory board again and stared at the names of the law firm. Cocharan, Thomas, Rand, and Kahill.

Kahill. Rand. Cocharan. Could it be? What would be in it for them without the association with another stockholder? Dennison had said that K.R.C. had no more to do with the Rands than it did with his own firm. Maybe there was more truth to that than he intended. But would he have simply handed her that big of a clue?

She needed to talk to someone, and Leo and his son would not be back until about one o'clock. She called Jim, hoping she wasn't waking him. He usually rose by ten or eleven after working the night shift. That would all change when he became a detective. Which would be just before their wedding. *Good timing*, she thought.

'Did I wake you?'

'No, Jenn. I've been up.'

'Hungry?'

'Yeah.'

'Let's kill two birds with one stone. I need help.'

They met at a popular luncheon spot where they found it nearly impossible to talk. They ate quickly and then sat in his car.

'You're right on the button,' Jim said. 'The problem is, Dennison's offer — on behalf of K.R.C. — *was* made before Samantha's death. But regardless, unless he was aware that the majority stock would fall from fifty to forty upon the execution of Samantha Stanton's will, the purchase doesn't make sense.'

'Unless he's just advising K.R.C. that the company will be run better now,' Jennifer suggested.

'But he couldn't have known of her death at the time of the offer.'

'Or could he?' Jennifer asked.

'Maybe as the representative of K.R.C., Conrad Dennison didn't know,' Jim said, warming to her idea. 'But K.R.C. knew, whoever they are.'

'Can we say that K.R.C. Limited is a suspect — at least one of their people — because they knew of the death in advance and assumed that it would make the sale more attractive?'

'It's a long shot,' Jim said, 'and the problem is that it points only to greed as a motive.'

'What's wrong with that? It's a solid enough motive, isn't it?'

'It's a little galling,' he said.

'Granted. But now how do we establish means and opportunity if we don't know who K.R.C. is?'

'We don't. But let's try something.'

Jennifer knew not to ask what Jim was up to

when he was in that mood with that look on his face. He liked surprises, and he also liked play-by-play announcing them as he went along.

About halfway downtown, he announced that they were going to speak with his soon-to-be superior, Detective Lieutenant Grady Luplo. 'He'll know if we have enough to get a warrant to search for the name in private records.'

'I implied to Dennison that I would find it in public records,' Jennifer said. 'But it would also be like looking for a needle in a haystack.'

'Were you bluffing, or did you really think you could find it?'

'I don't bluff, you know that.'

'Well, you weren't going to find it in public records, and Dennison probably knew that. Don't suppose he gave you much in exchange for that threat.'

'Matter of fact, he didn't.'

Grady Luplo was an interesting looking character who seemed to enjoy wearing his plainclothes suit, but wearing it less than tidily. The jacket was unbuttoned, and he stood with his hands jammed into the front pockets of his trousers.

'Wow,' he said, after a half hour of listening to Jennifer's story and Jim's question. 'I don't think so, Jim. No, you haven't nearly enough. There's an awful lot of speculation there, grasping for straws, you know what I mean. I mean, with her buying the drugs herself? I could call my buddy in the D.A.'s office, and he could look up the information for me without a warrant. It wouldn't be totally legal, but — '

'Then we don't want to do it,' Jennifer said earnestly.

'Now, wait a minute,' Jim said. 'I want to get this straight. Is it actually a crime for us just to *know* this information?'

'No,' Luplo said. 'It's a crime to use it.'

'Is it illegal for you or your friend to dig it out?'

'No. But it can't be used without cause. It'll be thrown out of court. You'll lose your case.'

'But the problem is, Lieutenant, that we could use the information to expose a murderer.'

'Yeah, you probably could. But if it ever came out that you got the information illegally, you've shot your case on a technicality.'

'What would make it legal?'

'The D.A. You want me to call him? I'll call him.'

Luplo spoke for several minutes with a contact in the District Attorney's office whom he called Larry. Larry dug out the information for him by computer and read the name to Luplo over the phone. 'Thanks, Larry,' he said. 'I'll probably have to talk to a judge before I can do anything with this, but I'll let you know.'

He hung up and turned back to the young couple. 'They gave me the name,' he said. 'I know what it stands for, but I really shouldn't tell you if you're going to pursue this.'

'What if we used the name to flush out the killer and got him to admit it himself?' Jim asked.

'Good question. But if it *ever* came out that you

got the information without due cause or a warrant, the case would be jeopardized.'

'Did you say name, singular?' Jennifer asked.

Luplo smiled. 'I did say that, didn't I?'

'Can you tell me if it's a man or a woman's name?'

'I can tell you that I don't recognize the name. You might, but I don't. It's not a usual name, and I have this feeling that I might have seen or heard it somewhere before, but it doesn't send off any rockets with me.'

'Ooh, this is frustrating!' Jennifer said. 'That name could be the name of the murderer, someone who had enough knowledge of the business and of Samantha Stanton's life that he or she could have pulled this off. But for what purpose? For what gain?'

'The D.A.'s office agrees we don't have enough, ma'am,' Lieutenant Luplo said. 'I can ask a judge directly, but they don't like going through us. They prefer their own kind.'

'Isn't there a judge in Chicago who was a cop once?' Jim asked.

'Yeah! There is. I'll try him if you want, but you know Saturday is a court holiday. He won't like being bothered at home.'

'How long will it take?' Jennifer asked.

'I'd prefer waiting until early afternoon,' he said.

'We'd better go, Jim. I've got to meet Leo.'

'Yeah. And lover boy Markie.'

'Oh, please.'

Leo was almost cheerful compared to how he had been before he'd gone to Wisconsin. He still had his teary moments, but mostly he was characterized by an attitude that signalled he was ready to get back into the fight.

Jennifer pulled him off to the side to apologize for opening his mail. 'Ah!' he said. 'It's all right. I was surprised, yeah, and the lawyer was ready to have you fired.'

'Really?'

'Yeah! But you know what? I told him to cool his jets. I told him I'd have done the same thing myself. We nosy journalists are all the same. Proves your qualifications.'

'It was still wrong, and I'm sorry,' she said.

'Granted,' he said. 'In truth, you owed me that apology, and I accept it.' He gave her a little hug. 'And I owe you an apology too, or I should say Mark does. You won't get one from him, so it'll have to come from me.'

'What are you talking about, Leo?'

'About the way he talked to you on the phone the other night. If he'd been younger, I'd have tanned his hide. He was humiliated to know I overheard him, but I gave him what for anyway. You won't have any more trouble from him.'

'Oh, it was all right, Leo. I'm flattered that he was — '

'Nonsense. He knew all along that you were both a widow and engaged. It was foolish and inappropriate, and I told him that. And I apologize.'

'I admit I got a little tired of it,' she said. 'Apology accepted.'

By the time she and Jim had filled Leo in on the progress of her investigation, Mark had called a cab and was waiting for his ride to the airport. He was sullen and hadn't looked Jennifer in the eye.

When the cab arrived, Leo stood and embraced his son, both crying. It was difficult for Leo to let go, but the cabbie was honking.

As Mark left, Jennifer thought she saw a look of apology on his face when he finally looked at her. So she smiled her forgiveness, hoping she was guessing right and praying he wouldn't misinterpret the smile.

'Timing,' Leo said, as he settled back into his chair. 'That's the key to all this stuff. I want to know what you found and when you found it. I'm tellin' you, Jennifer, you're going to get your break when you put it together in sequence and relate it to other events. You'd be surprised how the whys and the whens of what people do are related.'

Jennifer looked at Jim, wondering if Leo knew what he was saying. 'Well, boss,' she said, 'when I'm finished telling you what I've found, you may lose the equilibrium you gained with your rest.'

'Not good, huh?'

'Not all good, no. Some very confusing and troubling.'

He looked woefully at her. 'Some of it point to, ah, suicide?'

She nodded. He shook his head slowly. 'If it

makes any difference to you, Leo, Jim and I are still convinced it was murder.'

'Against heavy odds?' he asked.

He held his head in his hands as he heard what she had found at the pharmacies. He covered his mouth with his hand when he heard of the diabetes and the glaucoma. He wept when he heard of the meetings she attended.

'It just doesn't sound like her,' he said. 'Maybe hiding the illness from me. She was always considerate. But this other stuff. It's almost as if someone put her up to it. But nobody could ever put Sam up to anything she didn't want to do.'

He sat rocking back and forth, hands on his head. 'What in the world have you found to overcome all this evidence?'

She told him of her investigation into the travel agency business. He didn't brighten, but he seemed to listen intently. He agreed there might be something to the name, 'and my curiosity is killing me,' he said. 'When are they going to get back to you on that?'

'Any time,' Jim said. 'We hope soon, but if they don't think she's turned up enough evidence, they won't give it to us at all.'

'Are you kidding?' Leo said, 'Those cops are just like we are. They like a good fight. If they think there's anything in that name, they'll let it out. Either that or they'll go after it themselves.'

Realizing a cop was in the room, he winked at Jim. And the phone rang.

13 It was Lieutenant Grady Luplo, calling for Jim. He wanted Jim and Jennifer to come back downtown to talk to the judge.

Leo wanted to be in on everything. 'I'm tired of hibernating,' he said. 'Gotta get back in the game. Besides, I can sense you're onto something. This may not be fun, but I want to see it happen — whatever it is.'

On the way downtown, Leo wanted to know how Jennifer worked out the murderer planted the booklets. 'I was afraid you'd ask,' she said. 'That's the biggest stumper right now, along with the pharmacy purchases. It's apparent the pill was made up several days before Samantha died, based on when the ingredients were purchased.'

'But how do you explain her buying the ingredients, unless she was despondent over Dr. Billings's diagnosis?'

'I'm not sure of that either,' Jennifer said. 'Maybe she was forced to buy them, or maybe it wasn't really her. You see, Leo? There's a lot to overcome. I hope the judge doesn't ask the same questions.'

'You can bet he will, unless he's in a bad mood. Did they say which judge it was?'

'Ottomeyer,' Jim said.

'Crazy old coot,' Leo said. 'Funny, engaging guy, but coasting. He won't ask a thing, but he'll listen a lot. Be careful not to tell him more than you want to.'

Suddenly, Leo was tired. He leaned his head against the window of the back door and tried to sleep. 'I can't get past the booklets, the pharmacies, and the meetings,' he said. 'I want to believe what you believe, Jenn, but a gut feeling is all I have.'

'And timing,' Jim said. 'You said it yourself, Leo.'

Leo nodded.

Jennifer rifled through her notebook, comparing dates and times and places. 'Leo!' she shouted, making everyone jump. 'Samantha was out of the country when the pharmacy purchases were made! Why didn't I see that before?'

Stanton shuddered. 'I can hardly believe it,' he said. 'Even though it's staring me in the face. It *was* murder.' He shivered again. 'What a feeling,' he said, staring out the window. 'To think someone would do that to my wife.' He added quietly, 'Timing.'

Jennifer kept reading, flipping pages back and forth and making new notes. Leo grew sullen. 'I have to know who,' he said, 'legally or otherwise. If the judge won't give the police a warrant, I'll get your lieutenant friend to tell me anyway.'

'Leo — ' Jennifer said.

He held up a hand to silence her, as if to tell her not to even waste her breath.

Leo was right about the judge. He was full of jokes and wisecracks, but he did listen to Jennifer's story of the investigation.

'You'd make a good policewoman, anybody ever tell you that?' the old man cackled.

'My fiancé has told me many times.'

'This guy here? You a cop?'

'Yes, sir.'

'Good. A detective?'

'Soon,' Luplo said.

'Hire the woman instead,' the judge said, laughing. He slapped his palms onto his knees and rose unsteadily. 'All right,' he said, 'down to business.'

He motioned for Luplo to follow him out into the hall, and as they left, Jennifer heard him begin: 'Grady, I'm gonna get a warrant delivered to the D.A.'s office. Now you take over the thing from here and — '

When Luplo returned, he grinned slyly. 'Jim,' he said, 'you can come along on official business. Mr. Stanton and Mrs. Grey, if you're up to it, I need you as decoys.'

'Decoys?'

'Yes, ma'am. We may need you to role play to flush out the quarry.'

They mapped strategy in the car, and it was four in the afternoon when they arrived at the offices of the *Day*. On the way through the lobby, Jennifer tugged at Leo's sleeve. 'The drugs were purchased the day after your promotion was announced,' she said.

'Timing,' he whispered. 'I'm nervous.'

'Me too,' she said.

When they entered Leo's spacious office next to a conference room on the sixth floor, Luplo was introduced to the secretary, who explained how the intercom worked.

'Let's try it,' he said. 'Leo, you and Jennifer go into your office and talk in normal tones.' After a few seconds, 'Ah, that's good. Now, is there a way we can signal that office from out here?'

The secretary showed him a button that emitted a beep so innocuous that the occupants of the office would have to listen for it and know it was coming. 'Perfect,' he said. 'Make the call, Jennifer.'

'Mr. Roloff? Jennifer Grey. Fine, thank you, and you? Good. Listen, I'm doing a piece on Mrs. Stanton for the Sunday paper, and I was wondering if you knew whether your wife would be available for a few follow-up questions.'

'Follow-up questions?'

'You knew I interviewed her the other day?'

'Ah, no. No, I didn't. But, uh, she's coming to pick me up. We're going out tonight. She should be here any minute. When would you need to talk to her?'

'Right away, if possible, sir.'

'Well, we are going out.'

'So early? If I could just have, say thirty minutes, I could wrap this up and not have to come in tomorrow. Could you have her call me when she arrives? I'd appreciate it.'

There was a pause. 'I suppose so. You won't be long?'

'Not at all. In fact, Mr. Stanton's secretary has given me permission to use his office, so we'll have complete privacy.'

'Oh.'

'So she can reach me here. I just want the best friend angle, you understand.'

'Sure. I heard Leo had gone to Wisconsin. How's he doing?'

'Under the circumstances, I'd say as well as could be expected.'

'Uh-huh. Well, good. Good man. Need him back here. Hey, here's June now!'

'Thanks, Mr. Roloff. I'll be waiting in Mr. Stanton's office.'

Leo and Jim and Grady Luplo stepped into a conference room and waited for the secretary's signal that Mrs. Roloff was in with Jennifer. Then they stepped back into the outer office and had the secretary phone Kent Roloff again.

'Mr. Roloff, Mr. Stanton would like to see you in his office, please.'

'Leo's back?'

'Yes, sir.'

'I didn't know. I mean, when did he get back? Is he all right?'

'He returned this afternoon, and he seems to be doing fine. May I tell him you'll be right up, sir?'

'Absolutely. Is my wife up there?'

'Yes, sir.'

Roloff arrived buttoning his coat and straightening his tie. 'Leo, man, how are ya?' he said, shaking Leo's hand. 'I mean, *Mr. Stanton*, right? Gotta give the boss his due, don't I?'

Leo nodded and smiled weakly. 'Kent, this is Lieutenant Grady Luplo, Chicago PD. And you know Jim.'

'Nice to meet you — yeah, hi, Jim.' Jim nodded. Roloff was still trying to put it all together. 'You guys ride home from work together or something?'

'They're here on business, Kent,' Leo said. 'Let's have a seat right here, huh?'

'What's it all about, Leo? And where's June?'

Leo nodded to his secretary who pressed the button, privately signalling Jennifer that everyone was in place and simultaneously opening the intercom so the four men in the outer office could hear the conversation.

'So I'll start teaching the class on Tuesday nights, and I'm still debating whether to accept an offer to take over the travel agency.'

'Who made that offer?' Jennifer asked.

'Well, someone from their board, I guess. I suppose Leo would know him. I'd do it if he thought I should, I guess, but it's hard, you know, like I told you, with all the memories and everything.'

'Would you wear a red wig if you ran the agency?' Jennifer asked.

'Pardon me?'

'Would you try to look like Samantha? I mean, it sounds like you're trying to keep her alive by living her life for her.'

'I'm not sure what you're driving at,' June said, suddenly emotional, 'but it's not easy losing your best friend.'

'I don't imagine it's easy losing your wife to murder either,' Jennifer said.

'You still think it's murder?'

'We know.'

'We?'

'We. A serious mistake was made when the murderer bought the ingredients for the fatal dosage, posing as Mrs. Stanton, when Mrs. Stanton was out of the country.'

'Really?'

'Really. There was interesting timing there, Mrs. Roloff. It was right around the time of her husband's promotion. Remember when Leo was promoted?'

She nodded.

'Promoted right past your husband?'

'We didn't view it that way. Kent has been at this same level for many years and enjoys it. He's been passed over before. I mean, not passed over. We don't see it as being passed over.'

'Anyway, he has enough outside business interests, does he not?'

'Outside? Oh, I suppose. I don't get too much involved in that.'

'You don't? The Kent Roloff Company Limited owns a quarter of the stock of the Gateway Travel Agency. And if everything goes as planned, K.R.C. will purchase another twelve and a half per cent from Mr. Griffin. When Mrs. Stanton's will is executed, you stand to pick up another ten per cent, giving you majority control.'

Silence. In the outer office Kent Roloff leaped to his feet and had to be restrained from bursting through the door. He started to yell, but Jim Purcell wrapped his hand around Kent's mouth.

'One thing I can't work out, Mrs. Roloff,' Jennifer said. 'How you planted the booklets with such excellent timing. I've already worked out that it was you who went to all those SMS meetings, signing Samantha's name each time. And the one time you badgered her into going, *she* signed the phony Claudia Brown name, and you must have signed something else. I mean, you couldn't get away with signing her name right in front of her, could you?'

Mrs. Roloff licked her lips, but her eyes never wavered. 'You worked that out all by yourself, did you?'

Jennifer nodded.

'You get a gold star. You'll never prove anything.'

'When handwriting analysis is done, you'll be finished,' Jennifer said. 'And when the young boy in the pharmacy gets a look at you with a red wig. No, you were just a little too eager to have it all at once, you know that?

'You were so jealous, so envious of Samantha that even your friendship couldn't stop you. She always had the spotlight, because she was real. She never had your money, but she had grace you could never muster.

'She saw herself and everyone else as common people. She taught the class. She led the tours. She managed the agency. You were second fiddle. She had the talented and respected husband.

'And when he was promoted over your husband, that was the last straw. You took your knowledge of her illness and put it together with your knowledge of her habits, her shopping, her chemists, her doctor, and even her bag.

'When did you take the opportunity to plant the pill in the bottle, June? Was it when she had to leave the room for a minute and was trusting you to watch it, the way we do with the one person we know we can trust?

'Did you wait on pins and needles, and for how long, before she finally got enough headaches and got around to the fatal pill? Did you ever wonder if you should grab the bottle and change your mind?'

Mrs. Roloff shook her head. She had worked up tears the first time around. None were necessary now.

'C'mon,' Jennifer said. 'Tell me about the booklets. How did you plant them at just the right time?'

June Roloff sighed heavily. 'That was just

luck,' she said softly. 'I gave them to her about a week before and asked her to hold them for me because I knew Kent wouldn't want them in the house. He wouldn't even want to know I had them. She said Leo wouldn't either, but I said Kent had even been known to go through my bag. She said Leo had never once got near her bag, even when she asked him to bring her something from it. So she kept them for me in her bag. Twice she told me she was bringing them back, and I asked her to just wait another week.'

'She waited long enough, didn't she?' Jennifer said.

Mrs. Roloff nodded. 'Kent had nothing to do with this, you know.'

Jennifer flinched. 'Are you serious?'

'Yes. He didn't know I was getting ten per cent of the company. He knew I owned a quarter through the private corporation, and we kept that from the Stantons over the years. But everything else was on my own. He knew nothing of it.'

Jennifer shook her head in disbelief.

'Oh, it's true,' Mrs. Roloff said in a monotone, staring straight ahead. 'And you almost assessed it correctly too.'

'Almost?'

'Almost.'

'Where was I off?'

'The reasons.'

'Not jealousy?'

'Oh, I suppose so. But it was Leo I wanted, not Samantha's life. Not her beauty. Not her visibility. Not her job or her teaching or her travels. I wanted him.'

'Did he ever know that?'

'Never. I never had the nerve to make a pass at him. Too much character there. In him, not me.'

'How was this going to get Leo for you?'

'Oh, I was only halfway there when you stepped in.'

'You mean — ?'

'Uh-huh. Only half the job was done.'

'Your husband — ?'

She nodded. ' — would have been next.'

When Jennifer reached the outer office, she fell into Jim's arms. June Roloff walked past two weeping men, both slumped in chairs. And into the custody of Lieutenant Grady Luplo, Chicago PD.